MY STILLNESS

PAUL GRIFFITH

My Stillness

A NOVEL

THE VANGUARD PRESS, INC., NEW YORK

for Charles Blackburn

MY STILLNESS

CHAPTER

ONE

Although I am now too old to believe any human event has a beginning you can lay a finger on and say here and nowhere else must be where it began, I am persuaded by the strong feelings of memory that I can date the development, if not the birth, of my stillness from that Christmas morning, as white as ice or flowers, when I was eight and awoke earlier than anyone else in our house to discover that the night had turned our suburban world into the continent of Antarctica.

It had snowed. And such a snow, which was being blown as high as my third-floor windows, was silent enough to rouse me at dawn. Its ghostly presence outside, its riffling and ruffling so oddly premonitory of Miss N. P. Kopestonsky and her taffeta gowns, its colorless yet penetrating glare forecasting the troubled glance of her Slavic eye, added to the uneasiness that was the daily tenor of those days in my life, child though I was.

Unable to go back to sleep beneath my quilts, I got up and shut my five windows. The views they offered—between transparent curtains just laundered and ironed for the holidays—were horizonless, extending into a sky undifferentiated except by some birds, some sparrows scattering like leaves. I looked at the yard directly below me. It was white, dead, still. I shivered. I made up my mind to go downstairs and find out whether or not my greatest fear, as I then regarded it, had come true.

My fear was that nothing had been left for me under the Christmas tree by my father—a fear not wholly unfounded in light of his recent behavior toward me, toward (I now can see) all of us—Mother and my brother Hughie, too.

Slipperless, I went down the three flights of newly waxed, yellow oak stairs and passed through the living room, which had the dim and tedious air of a Sunday when no company was expected. I passed through the hall littered with blue cardboard cartons from John Wanamaker's department store. I entered the dining room. . . . And there stood the Christmas tree, a bigger one than we had ever had when we lived above my father's office in town, a spruce that touched the ceiling, as high as the sky, its blackgreen branches hung with tinsel like webs, silver and gold, that looked vast enough to trap a child; its recently purchased, mostly red ornaments watching me and gleaming at me like the eyes of unknown creatures in its crooks and

8

crotches. In the scarily toneless light from the snow it loomed and reached for me.

There were other frightful things to be faced. At the tree's cotton-swathed, silver-sprinkled base lay the Christmas presents. There were a lot of them—too many for only us three. Getting down on my hands and knees, I sorted them into three piles, one for each. As I picked among them, I read the tags attached: "Hughie from Mommy," "Charlie J from Mommy," "Mommy from Charles," and so forth, until, with an evaporation of dread that I can compare to nothing nowadays except the relief offered by the new tranquillizing drugs, I held in my hand one tag that read: "Charlie J from Dad." Joy jetted through me like a fountain.

It didn't last. In the next instant I recognized—on the tag bordered with reindeer silver and red—my mother's baldly undisguised handwriting. I saw through her duplicity. I recalled her ambition, which, ungovernable spy and eavesdropper that I was, I had overheard her confide to one of her friends in a red fox fur, of wanting to become both mother and daddy to her "poor, fatherless boys." Knowing in my heart the futility of this aim of hers, scorning her for deluding herself about the very possibility of it, and hating her for trying to fool me, I laid aside the gift. I did not finish sorting the others. The piles I had created I disarranged so that no one could guess my curiosity about them. My fear had come true: there was, and would be, no present from my father.

On tiptoe, as though I felt guilty for my disappointment, I went back upstairs. I slipped into Hughie's frozen room and climbed into bed with him, lying as close as I could to the warm, insensible little body in pale-gray pajamas as soft as a kitten's coat. Eighteen months younger than I, he was a deep sleeper. The heat of our fraternal cave, to which I regularly fled on the darkest and most terrible nights as well as on the loneliest mornings, lulled me finally into another faint of unconsciousness. My mother, child-sized in her double bed on the floor below us, also slept on. It was as though none of us wanted to rouse ourselves to spend that holiday in exile in our pretty new house in the country.

Now, with the hindsight afforded me by forty years, I am able to guess the suffering endured by my brother and my mother during the wretched times I am describing. No doubt because I was then not at all sensitive to them, I have no memory whatever of Hughie's feelings. He was a rival of mine, a pest, a stubborn little troublemaker, whom I barred so effectively from my awareness, that most of the time he does not appear to have been present in that nine-room house on a one-acre lot. Of my mother, however, I still keep in my head many pictures—out in her garden, on the front porch, in the kitchen, and elsewhere—from which I can easily if painfully deduce her dumfounded misery. But I understood best the feelings of my Aunt Margaret, who was also there. And this memoir is essentially her story, as seen coincidentally through the slanting slits of my own eyes, so similar in their shape, if not their color or angle of vision, to hers. My eyes were hazel and as sharp as opera glasses. Hers were black and myopic. I do not think I ever noticed their blackness and strangeness, which gave her the appearance of a prosperous fortuneteller, until she arrived without warning on that chill Christmas morning.

That morning, when I awoke for the second time, Hughie had left the bed; our cave was beginning to lose its warmth through chinks in the blankets, and the front-door bell was ringing. It rang as softly as the bells of the white campanile on the snow-white grounds of the Roman Catholic seminary at the end of our street, as softly and politely and whitely as my father's voice speaking to a patient on the telephone.

I leaped out of bed and dashed down the stairs, assuring myself, as I skidded and stumbled, that since my father had not once visited our house after we moved into it, it must be he—and only he—who would be ringing our doorbell this particular day. I flew around the ninety-degree angles of the landings. I scattered Mother's little oriental throw rugs. I turned the large, well-polished brass key in the door to the vestibule, and then came to a halt of chagrin, of hope betrayed again. For above me, in the glass upper half of the front door, wreathed in ferns and flowers of ice and frost and wind-hurled snow, several blue-white plumes aflutter like a halo disintegrating on her snow-dotted black hair, yet as grand looking and as poised and posed as the subject of a portrait in oils, glared my Aunt Margaret.

I write "glared." But glaring was not characteristic of Aunt Margaret. As a matter of fact, I was to see her glare —by which I mean the focusing and beaming of all a person's hatred in his or her eyes—only once, and then only at the awful moment of her final breakdown out on our sunlit front lawn on the morning of July fifth, still more than six months away. I therefore must have been the one who glared and by some odd discombobulation of the mind have transferred it and the guilt of it to her eyes. That was the instant, anyhow, when I first noticed their blackness, their peculiar filminess, the impression they gave of seeing right through you to things and perhaps even persons of greater interest and importance. And their expression—if I press my memory, I can observe it correctly—was that of acute physical pain. The cause of her pain was elicited from her as soon as she strode into our house and my kimono-clad mother, always somewhat afraid of her but solicitous by nature of anyone sick, injured, or in trouble, came downstairs and started to take care of her.

Wrapped in khaki army blankets and propped up in the mulberry-upholstered wing chair next to the radiator, her bare yellow-toed feet cushioned on a pair of tomato-colored hot-water bottles, swallowing turkey broth and coffee as hot as she could stand them, Aunt Margaret told without self-pity but also without humor (she had no humor whatever) how her feet and her legs had come to be all frozen, her arms and gloveless hands the same, and what had happened to her luggage, her purse, and her good fur coat. . . .

"Your *good* one?" said my mother, who was not yet accustomed to my father's wealth or indeed to anyone's having any. "You have *two* fur coats, Margaret?"

"Three," said my aunt. "But this was the Alaskan seal Jean Phillips gave me in Paris."

"If I know you, Margaret," said my mother, who was very intelligent for all her naiveté and little-girl ups-and-downs, "if I know you, Margaret, you *gave* the coat away."

"I did," said my aunt. Without boasting but with, of course, that unabashed sense of her own uniqueness and special worth that is a trait of our family on my father's side, she proceeded to tell her story. She had gotten off the train at the wrong station, at North Philadelphia instead of Broad Street in town. The snowstorm, her bad eyesight, a careless conductor—who knows what or who was to blame? On the station platform, which is elevated high above the street, she had felt the storm breaking over her like waves of the Atlantic during a winter crossing, like waves of the typhoon she had once weathered on the Pacific. Everything on the platform was so windblown, white, and cold, she had imagined she was back in Russia, traveling again with Jean Phillips. In the breakers of snow she had not been able to find a porter to help or even direct her. Unable to lift the two suitcases in which she had been bringing us as Christmas presents some tracts and other publications by her indefatigable hand, she had simply sat down on one of the benches on the platform. "The Lord helps those who help themselves, I know," she said, "and I wondered at myself until I understood His purpose in allowing me to despair like that." For there, on the very bench on which she was sitting, she discovered—huddled like a drift—an old woman. Very old. "As old," she said, "as Mama the last time I saw her before going abroad with Jean." Wearing nothing but a dress and some newspapers that she was attempting with raw hands to use as a blanket, the old woman was freezing to death. Seeing her, my Aunt Margaret knew her Christian duty—and, being my Aunt Margaret, did it. She placed her coat, "good" though it was, around the old lady's shoulders. The effect of her charity was remarkable, almost instantaneous. The old woman stopped her shuddering, God-blessed my aunt, and tottered off, in the Alaskan seal from Paris, into the oceanic storm.

Whereupon my aunt turned around to try once again to lift her suitcases, only to find that they, along with her purse that she had set down and her white kid gloves she had to remove in order to perform her act of generosity, had, all of them, disappeared.

"Someone stole them," said my mother. "The old woman was in cahoots with him."

"Oh, no, Star," said my aunt. "The Lord would not allow such a dirty trick to be played on me."

Her flat, swift, indignant rejection of the obvious truth cowed my mother, who did not pursue it any further than to ask how, minus her coat, gloves, and purse, she had managed to arrive at our house on the other side of the city, a distance through the deepening snow of certainly five or six miles.

"I hiked," said my aunt.

No matter that her feet looked as if they had been boiled or that her hands were bleeding as if they had been slashed by knives of ice, Aunt Margaret had done right—or, as it invariably appeared in her tracts, Right. She had done her Duty. She had paid her Obligation to Him. The sensation of her own goodness lifted her beyond mere bodily discomfort. She would not permit my mother to call the doctor. After she had been warmed by several cups of hot liquids and an hour's monologue in our well-heated living room, she threw aside the army blankets and stood up, insisting she felt fine, never better, even though she limped and, I noticed, favored her left hand over her right, which was the bloodier.

"It's Christmas, the Lord's birthday," she said, "and I don't want to spoil it for Him or for the boys either."

Her handsome if too yellow face, the startling tone and

porcelain smoothness of which I childishly connected with her travels in the Far East, radiated a happiness that proved her imperviousness to physical pain. Her Tartar eyes glittered above Tartar cheekbones. Her black hair, on which she still wore that tricorn of bluish feathers now limply damp, shone like a crown of jet. She crossed the living room and, with a gesture singularly imperial, opened the double doors to the dining room.

It is that instant which I recall more clearly than the tale of her walk through the snow. Because, as she parted the apple-green doors, there was wafted to my nostrils an odor—greener than the paint, resinous and pure—that was the smell of the Christmas tree with its strings of many-colored lights turned on. Somehow, probably because of my curiosity about her and her exotic life, I confused it with the scent of her person. No doubt this was some extravagantly costly perfume presented to her by her friend Jean Phillips in, say, Hong Kong, Bombay, Moscow, or Mombasa. But the two real odors intermingled in my hypersensitive nostrils to manufacture an imaginary incense as odd and intensely interesting to me as the atmosphere of a Greek Orthodox cathedral or the peculiarly Persian reek of the interior of my mother's enamel cigarette box on the coffee table. And to this day I am not convinced it was a mixture of real odors at all but rather the peculiar physical emanation, recorded about the persons of ancient saints, that is usually described as possessing the sweetness of lilies or roses or violets but, whatever, is understood by all witnesses to be the actual olfactory sign of sanctity.

I must make it clear from the start of Aunt Margaret's story that I regard her as a true saint, the genuine God-stricken article, even though in the course of the events

15

I am about to relate she worked no miracle, unless the creation of my stillness was one, and she had occasion—indeed, several occasions—to act like a devil and leave in the wake of her infrangible predestination many victims, everybody involved, as a matter of record, except myself.

Thanks to her arrival, my mother, Hughie, and I were able to get through that Christmas Day under the pretense that all was well. By her own example Aunt Margaret commanded us to.

Toward the end of the afternoon, when the sky had turned as green as pond ice, and the four of us were lolling at the dining-room table with its litter of bone dishes full of brown-dappled turkey bones and slices of fruitcake, the front-door bell rang a second time.

Our pseudobliss disappeared. Hope ruined my mother's prettily white-powdered face, which she quickly hid behind her linen napkin. I felt sickish; Hughie ran to the door. Like our pet cardinals waiting for their daily ration of breadcrumbs and suet on the rhododendrons outside, the hopes of all three of us—of, I suspect, all four—had been there, unmentioned, throughout our feast.

"It's a present!" Hughie cried. "It's a present!"

A present. Not my father. Yet, I thought, the present had to be from him and it might—it must—be for me. I am sure my mother, behind her clutch of linen, shared the same disappointment and the same selfish hope for herself. We waited and stared while Hughie, small and fat for his age, staggered in with the belated gift. It was heavy, tall, and wrapped in plain white paper tied with common white string. Only Hughie's own hopes of its being for him —hopes that I considered detestable, preposterous, and frighteningly possible—provided him strength enough to raise the gift to the height of the table and set it at my mother's place.

Her tiny fingers, which seemed to be wearing white gloves for the purpose, untied the string and then began to unpeel the paper. The gift turned out to be a poinsettia. A white one held erect under our troubled gazing by several green-dyed stakes. Attached to one of the stakes, which leaned outward as if from the weight of its significance, was an envelope.

I can still see my mother's fingers opening that envelope and taking out the enclosed card as correctly as if she were selecting a canapé from a silver tray at Jean Phillips's home overlooking the Hudson; or rather, to be more accurate, since so many things happened that she was never to be invited to a party there, as if she were taking a square of crustless bread at communion in the Presbyterian church where she regularly attended both the morning and the evening services. She read the card. Then she completely covered her face with her napkin and began to cry in a silence like that of the snow outside. The card slipped from her hand on which she wore my father's seed-sized diamond.

My aunt picked up the card, scanned it, and deposited it inside her bosom, which was as yellow as her face.

Only later, when I was supposed to be asleep in my bed on the third floor, and my mother and Aunt Margaret were washing dishes, did I find out what the card said. I crept down the back staircase, which gave onto the kitchen, and learned that the card bore nothing but my father's first name—Charles—and had been signed not by his hand but someone else's, a stranger's. Moreover, my mother and aunt had managed to make out, perhaps from some telltale code on the card, the envelope, or the wrappings, or as the result of direct inquiry by telephone to Western Union, that the order for the poinsettia had originated not in town, where my father had been supposed by all of us to be spending the day at work in his office, but in Indianapolis. I can still hear my mother pronouncing the word: "Indianapolis!" On her lips it sounded awesome and terrible, like the name of one of the places in antiquity where human sacrifices were made.

"That's where Nina is," she said.

"Nina?" said my aunt. "My Nina?"

"Yes, Margaret. Your Nina is now my Charlie's!"

After that revelation, which, since I was not then acquainted with the woman called Nina, meant nothing to me except that someone other than my mother was in possession of my father, I am not certain what the two women said. Alternately they whispered and cried out over the rattle of china and glassware and silver and the running of water. They took turns weeping and comforting each other down there. Their adult distress terrified me.

Yet almost without my knowledge, I was soothed by my aunt's speaking voice, a contralto with a high, shimmery ring to it like that, I imagine, of the golden trumpets of heaven about which she would soon be telling me. She was trying to calm Mother. She said the good Lord would not let a single event happen upon this earth unless, in the long run, it did not turn out for the best. Everything was for the best. She repeated the phrase as though it were the refrain of her favorite hymn, either "I Walk in the Garden Alone" or "Bringing in the Sheaves," which, once she was

18

settled in the house with us, she would hum perpetually.

"Oh, but Margaret!" my mother wailed: "Indianapolis! Indianapolis!" She could not endure the very name of the city in which Nina lived.

To me, in my cramped and guilty position in the darkness against the wall, Aunt Margaret was persuasive. I believed her, as in the past so many people of so many colors in so many places around the world had apparently been obliged to believe her, all her colorful words golden or pearly or rosy or shining. Whatever she sang in that triumphant voice, with that angelic confidence of hers, had to be true.

"Indianapolis!"

But I, lulled, entranced, converted, fell asleep where I was.

After Christmas, instead of returning to share Jean Phillips's nomadic life, Aunt Margaret stayed with us. Only later did I learn that, having had apparently more than words with her dearest friend and patroness, the publisher of all her tracts and allegorical poems, she actually had nowhere else to flee to, and that, even if she had such a sanctuary, she could not come up with the wherewithal to get there. I should guess also that Mother begged her to stay. So orphaned by my father's abandonment of us, so lonely, distraught, and young (she was thirty-three, but she seemed only the eldest of us children), my mother had no one else to turn to. It was advantageous that each woman should pass through the crisis of her life with the solace of a companion, no matter how dissimilar from herself. My mother said, "Margaret needs a home, someone to cook for her, mend her stockings, sew on buttons." My aunt's stated purpose in remaining with us was to reunite my mother and father.

"It's got to be, Star. It's simply got to be," she said. "Now I know why I felt I could not go on with Jean a moment longer. The Lord wanted me here with you and the boys. He knows I can get you and Charles back together again."

"But what about Nina?"

"He will take care of her, have no doubt about that," my aunt said. "Just how, I don't know yet. But He will," she insisted. "Everything's always for the best."

They talked in whispers, in passionate conferences, in female cries stifled for Hughie's and my sake every night. And every night I eavesdropped from the back staircase. Their effort to keep their voices down was brief. It was never long before my mother's feelings of injury, self-pity, or panic, or my aunt's fierce rebuttals, raised their discussion to a pitch of mutual consternation that I did not have to hold my breath to catch. Occasionally, very occasionally, this did not happen until late, three-thirty or four in the morning. Once it did not happen until five, chilly and still, the safety of night's blackness spoiled by a nerve-wracking infusion of dawn and the pale chirping of birds. Whenever it happened, though, it was always the same. My mother would sob. My aunt would denounce Nina Kopestonsky, the weakness of the male character, the city of Indianapolis, everything in creation except the Creator Himself. On and on they went, venting, between them, the opposite limits of my own emotions, the weakness of my despair and the strength of my outrage at having been cast out by my father, until even my vicarious satisfaction was complete and I sneaked upstairs to bed. Often, as I snuggled in next to Hughie, I could still hear them. There were many nights when none of us slept at all.

"The whole thing's my fault," my aunt said.

"Oh, Margaret, how can you say that?"

"It is. I brought it about. In all innocence, of course. But I brought it about." My aunt assumed full responsibility for Nina Kopestonsky's capture of my father, since it was she who had first directed her and her always mysterious ailments to his office. Miss Kopestonsky had—or had had—something wrong with one of her legs. Whatever it was, it had forced her to abandon the cause for the advancement of which my aunt and Jean Phillips had spent seven years traveling around the world. As I recall those discussions of Miss Kopestonsky's afflicted member, which were as unflinchingly detailed as if the subject were a cow's dry bag or a pig's colic (both my mother and my aunt were country women, after all, and spoke more frankly than is common in Philadelphia), I realize that Miss Kopestonsky must have suffered the disease called phlebitis—and no wonder, considering how as secretary, colporteur, and general factotum, she had tried to keep up with my aunt and her equally fanatic friend and patroness, weathering the Atlantic, the Pacific, and many other bodies of water, traipsing through China, India, and innumerable mission stations in Africa, yielding only when her leg did, which happened at the moment ("very inconvenient") when the three of them were setting out for Moscow to convert the Bolsheviks. She had come home "on furlough" then and, following my aunt's proud suggestion, had consulted my father about her leg.

"It turned purple," my aunt said.

Listening, I pictured Miss Kopestonsky as nothing but

her highly colored leg, as distorted as some modern paintings. I envisioned her presenting it in its rotten state to my father. I imagined his hands, which were the cleanest I ever saw, taking it—so disturbing a sight, so ugly. And in reality Miss Kopestonsky could not be described as a beauty. She was too tall, too thin, too toothy. I was to discover these facts for myself at a later date, but I first heard them during that first week of Aunt Margaret's stay, between Christmas and New Year's, because my mother wanted to know everything there was to be known about her, and my aunt desired even more, or so it sounded to me, to assess her—her pluses, as she said, and her minuses.

My aunt said, "Nina Kopestonsky was never what you and I would call a good-looking woman. Definitely not. But she had a certain *je ne sais quoi*. I'll hand her that."

My mother wept at this judgment of Miss Kopestonsky. She wept over her virtues even more, it struck me, than over her faults. She wept copiously and nightly.

It was when my aunt attempted to soothe my mother that she spoke most firmly. "You must have faith, Star," she said. "The Good Lord would not permit an awful thing like this to happen if He did not have a purpose in it. A purpose far beyond your ken, Star. Yes, and beyond mine, too. You will just have to wait until He makes it clear to you. And He will; I know He will. There will come a Day when the heavens will open and the golden trumpets will sound, and the golden stairs will descend, and down will come His messenger, bearing His message to you. And on that Day, at last, All will become as clear to you as the sun itself."

At these times my aunt's voice grew elocutionary and her language semi-Biblical, studded with pearls and other precious jewels. She spoke in the same style in which, as I was to find out, she composed her tracts, poems, and fourteen-page personal letters. Delivered by her deep and vibrantly sincere voice, her words were not only convincing but beautiful, as beautiful to me as a lullaby sung by a stranger to an orphan in the dark. Sometimes, while I crouched on my secret step on the back stairs, they seemed to be inscribed in fire upon the motionless air of our chilly house.

My mother was neither impressed nor calmed by these sermons. Either she went on crying right through them or she refused to take them seriously. She could behave surprisingly flippantly. For instance, to the exhortation recorded above, that she wait for "a Day," she said, "Margaret, you make it sound as if I were going to be pregnant again."

Not realizing that my mother was only protecting herself from the pain of still another hopeless hope, my aunt said, "Star, it is not like you to blaspheme."

And this, naturally, set off a small girl's tantrum of more sobs and wails.

My aunt stopped the tantrum by handing my mother a tea towel to dry her face and by referring again to her own determination to bring my father home.

My mother said, "Oh, Margaret, if I could only believe in what you say!"

"Believe in Him," said my aunt.

The two of them, robust with misery, were able to stand the strain of those nocturnal conversations. I, mute and afraid, was worn out by them. One night, after they had gone on chattering even later and more strenuously than was their habit, like a pair of canaries left uncovered in their cage, I again fell asleep at my post on the back stairs. On this particular night my mother must have gone up to bed before my aunt, as she did on occasion in order to take a pill and lie down with a dampened washrag on her forehead. This, anyway, would explain how it was that my aunt climbed up the back stairs and in the darkness found me. Kicked me, in fact, with the stub toe of her practical low-heeled shoe. She startled me so that instantly I supposed I was being punished for my inveterate spying and prying. Because I did not immediately know who was administering the punishment—all I could make out was a large solidity, blacker than the black surrounding me—and because I felt so guilty, I began to sob. I am certain the sobs were loud because of my aunt's response. She got angry. She reached down into the darkness, as into a flood of water, and gathered me up in her arms as if to stifle me. Indeed, at first I thought they were my father's arms. Whereupon, with a roughness that seemed tender as well as irritable, they cradled me and pressed me against a chest as hard-boned as a man's that nevertheless gave off a scent I had enjoyed before, and proceeded to carry me downstairs. The only words uttered to me in the course of this cautious journey down the invisibly curved and precipitous steps were a decrescendo, from deep to deeper, from soft to softer, of the same two words: *"Be still!* Be still! Be still. Be still. . . ."

They failed to stop my crying. The nightly dialogue of my mother and my aunt had brought my nervous system to such a state of tension that nothing but a direct statement by myself—this babyish yelling—could relieve it. I cried as

I had wanted to cry since that day, early in September, when we moved to our new house in the suburbs in time for the opening of school and I deduced from my mother's open face, and eventually from a phone call to which I listened on the extension upstairs, that my father would not be joining us. "Never," he said, "never, Star. Never."

I lay in my aunt's strong arms and at last let it out: the unhappiness that, I see now, I would not express to my mother because she had enough of her own to hide behind her linen napkins, handkerchiefs, and tea towels; the unhappiness I could not share with Hughie because he was too little to understand, or so the lady in the red fox fur had said; the unhappiness I would not admit even to myself because I was too proud and would no more permit myself to weep over my father's abandonment of me than I would over his furious, sometimes violent wielding of the ivory-handled hairbrush on my bare backside—I refused to give him the satisfaction.

While I cried, my aunt carried me, a boy big for my age, through the unoccupied rooms of the first floor of our house, holding me in front of first this window and then that, where the ending of the night in a pale unclean dawn, the same color as a newly laid egg in Grandma Thomas's chicken coop, only doubled my horror at the world's increasing whiteness, its awful emptiness.

She held me for many minutes, for an hour, perhaps longer. Over and over again she sang into my ear the same oddly lovely phrase—"Be still. Be still"—until finally, like the meaning of a kiss, it penetrated the barriers of my skin and flesh and set me to weary rest.

When I was quiet, she sat me down at the dining-room

table and gave me a glass of milk and a box of graham crackers. She did not sit down with me. She paced. She hummed "I Walk in the Garden Alone." She rubbed her hands from which the bandages had only recently been removed. Suddenly, in the nastily brightening light of another day, she stood still and looked at me hard. "What am I going to do with you, child?" she said. "Shall we take down the Christmas tree? Untrim it?"

"Oh, can we?"

"It ought to have been taken down weeks ago. It's a sight. Or should I put you to bed?"

"Let's take it down and surprise Mother!"

"All right. Let's surprise Mother. Quietly now. Easy does it."

Standing precariously on one of the dining-room chairs, my aunt took off the tree's ornaments. I, beginning at the prickly branches that touched the floor, unwound the webs of tinsel. Because of my mother's lack of Christmas spirit, the tree had been but sparsely decorated to begin with, and we did not take long to strip it bare. Leaning lopsidedly, it looked like a cripple, like an old woman who was losing her hair. I felt sorry for the tree, for its incurable death, just as, when I was younger, still a baby, I used to sympathize to the point of tears with flowers whose heads had been snipped off to fill my mother's vases, seeing not a skilled and sumptuous arrangement but a mass execution.

When my aunt suggested that she and I lug the tree through the French doors from the dining room to the porch, and that we burn it in the front yard, I was delighted. I had never before been permitted to burn a tree.

I held the doors open. My aunt, as strong as a man, hoisted the tree to one shoulder and carried it outside, throwing it in a single sweeping gesture from the porch into the yard's deep snow, still white, even after so much time since Christmas Day.

Abandoned there, the tree attracted more of my pity. This feeling must have puckered my features, for my aunt said almost crossly, "Go fetch the matches, child."

I did, and when I came back from the kitchen I found she had already set the tree upright in the snow so that it appeared to be half alive again. She took one of the blue-tipped matches, struck it, and held it to a lower branch. It caught at once. Flames rose directly upward, blue and then yellow and then orange—the fanciest Christmas-tree decorations I ever saw. The entire tree was aglint with fire —like, I thought, someone wicked in the Bible being punished by the hand of God Almighty. It was as disturbing as it was beautiful: I felt as if I myself were being consumed by fire. Yet, as I reached for my aunt's rough-skinned hand, I saw the morning's sun rise and begin to burn too, among the icy branches of all the other, taller unlighted trees. The whole world was burning. I had no doubt it was the Day of Judgment about which I had, of late, overheard so much from my listening post on the back stairs. My aunt's hand, which, on account of its frost-bite, must have still been painful to use, exerted a slight pressure on my own, and she said, "Charlie J, I promise you one thing. We'll go to town and have a talk with your daddy and bring him home." I was not at all surprised. I always believed everything she said. I took every word of hers literally. My trust was so complete that I thought the Almighty had deliberately chosen her to bring me His message of hope, instead of the ethereal creature with an Easter lily in his hand whom I had been expecting for days and days.

CHAPTER

TWO

From the fiery moment when my aunt gave me her promise—as much from an old maid's exasperation with a neurotic child, I have no doubt, as from any real intention—I began to be impatient.

I expected her promise to be kept immediately, that night or the next or the next after that, but never more than forty-eight hours away, which was the limit of my hope. My bad habit of twisting my cowlick became a tic. The tiny screw of black hair, not a third as long as a Chinaman's pigtail, stood up on the crown of my head like a prepubescent erection. In addition, I pulled at my lower lip until it turned into a raw, red sore.

Aunt Margaret's promise was to be kept eventually in the most drastic, devious, and violent ways. But it was not kept at once. It was not kept until late February.

In the meantime she worked. She had a typewriter that had been forwarded after Christmas, along with her clothes, in two enormous steamer trunks that bore the initials "J.P." among the bright confetti-like remnants of foreign labels pasted all over them. She placed the typewriter on a card table (which she strongly objected to my mother's possessing) before the front window of her bedroom. She put a straight chair at the table, and from the instant I awoke in the morning until my mother summoned us all to dinner ("Time to eat, everybody!") she was seated in the chair and typing. The table legs did a tap dance on the floor.

She worked like the fanatic she was, like a drudge, like a nun—like, in fact, my father. Bent toward the large and rusty typewriter, as huge to my eyes as an automobile engine, she wore while she worked only a ragged unmended slip, always the same one of dirty-looking, unpressed pink silk. Also, her hair was unpinned, covering her completely from head to heel like a habit or garb of the prescribed black—black velvet, though, rather than any ascetic homespun. Her toes, with their untrimmed nails and strangely oriental tint, like imported marble, were bare and upright, poised rigidly, like a pianist's at the pedal. Her brown tortoise-shell glasses, frequently misted by the passion and duration of her intellectual labors, clung to the bump on the prominent bridge of her somewhat lengthy, too pointy nose. Her fingers now rushed at the typewriter keys, now poked at them, now paused over them, cruising the air like hawks on the verge of swooping to the kill: they never rested. They did not linger when a page had been completed. She neither sat back and reread and felt satisfied by her compositions nor—that I ever saw—suffered dissatisfaction. She made no corrections—I suppose because she believed the Lord had written each page through her, had employed her hand to shape the word as Miss Arnold used to do with mine in first grade, had spoken through her as ghosts do through the lips of mediums. I understand her only in retrospect. How could she, His amanuensis, presume either to appraise or change one of the words so put down?

Whoever their author, however, the pages—black with type and all but marginless—were plentiful. They littered the card table, the floor, the surfaces of the radiator, the dresser, the mantel, the forever-unmade bed. They were her tracts. She turned out one a day. I have one in my possession still. Entitled "A Tool In His Hand," it is couched in the pretentious and cliché-spotted language of her nightly exhortations to my mother in the kitchen, but far less charitable. Its high-and-mightiness, as a matter of fact, amazes me. I am surprised, too, by its irrelevancies—animadversions as strict as curses on cardplaying, dancing, and the use of tobacco. In addition to the tracts, my aunt also produced letters, tens and twenties and thirties of them daily, although insofar as I can remember she did not during her stay with us receive a single one in return.

And then one February afternoon I came home from school with my customary reluctance and Mother said, "Go upstairs and put on your Sunday suit. Your aunt is taking you to dinner with your daddy tonight."

Aunt Margaret's promise was to be kept at last. Hope tingled through my skinny body. Yet my reply turned out to be: "What about my homework?"

"You don't have to do homework when there's something more important to do, when you're invited to your daddy's for dinner. I'll write Miss Gravdahl a note."

"I'm invited?"

"Yes, your aunt arranged it."

"Was Hughie invited, too?"

"No. Hughie's too little."

And so, after I had dressed, and the snow, which had not yet entirely melted, had turned violet, and the sun looked like a Christmas tree being burned on a faraway slope of the slushy gray sky, my aunt's promise came true.

I was dressed and ready to go before my aunt was. When she came down the front staircase, she wore one of the apparently numberless hand-me-downs that her friend Jean Phillips had sent in the pair of battered steamer trunks.

We were impressed, my mother by the high fashion of this hitherto unseen garment, I by its many colors that made me think of Joseph and his coat, my favorite story in the Bible. The gorgeousness of the colors, rainbowing from delphinium-blue through yellow to reds of all shades —from pink to rose to scarlet to magenta to purple—hung about her like a sunset mist, like her celestial perfume materialized. But it was her hat that roused the most enthusiasm in me. An extravaganza of gleaming reds and glowing blues, downwardly bewinged by a pair of long red feathers with black tips, it looked like the crown of a barbaric queen, Hawaiian or perhaps Polynesian. Seeing it, I knew I could not share my mother's doubts, occasionally confided to me in the guiltiest whispers, as to the strict truthfulness of my aunt's tales about her travels and the impressive list of acquaintances she claimed to have struck up on them—Mahatma Gandhi, for example, and many countesses.

My aunt was thoroughly conscious of the effect her costume was making. Descending the stairs slowly, each red satin slipper performing solo, one white-gloved hand gracing the ruddy mahogany of the banisters, hair sleek, her eyes like flashy jewels, she posed for our benefit, saying nothing to distract us from our stares.

Once downstairs, she remained mute. Like an actress or an empress, she wrapped herself in her second-best coat, shinily black and reaching to her thickish ankles. As I recall the event, which is the only word adequate to her appearance that night, I realize how enured she was to being ogled by the world. I see that, writer and public speaker, the constant companion of a well-known heiress, she was a personage. She could no more have avoided distinction than could my father. Dressed up in Jean Phillips's old clothes, she was an eye-catching woman, a somebody, if neither really beautiful nor smart.

My mother, pretty in a much smaller and more private style, like a cameo next to a topaze or ruby, looked up at her and said, "Oh, Margaret! If I had your looks, maybe people'd stop glaring at me out here in the suburbs as if I were a nobody trying to worm my way in!"

My aunt made one of her royal gestures with her hands. "Well, Star, when I get home tonight, you may have the coat for your very own," she said, as though the coat were the sole ingredient in her gaudy magnificence.

"Oh, Margaret, I simply couldn't!"

"I have another."

"Well, it will have to be cut down drastically."

My mother: "Give your father a hug and a great big kiss for me too!" Whereupon she pressed to mine her perfectly shaped mouth, as pink as a doll's, and gave me a kiss that—since it was meant for you-know-who instead of me—I did not respond to.

Because she was "afraid" of running into my father, my mother did not drive us into Philadelphia that evening. Aunt Margaret called a Yellow Cab.

It seemed strange to be deposited like a new patient at the house on Chestnut Street, all red brick and tall windows, where we had always lived until our move to the suburbs. Strange because, since the move, which had brought about our unexpected exile, the house appeared to have grown larger, wider, higher. Strange because it had, in fact, been renovated, its front porch removed as totally as if by surgery, its windows trimmed with shutters that were only for looks and would not shut, a white Georgian door added, and, next to the door, the bronze plaque bearing my father's name and medical degree (he called it his "shingle") polished so that it gleamed, in the still-wintry twilight of that evening, with golden glory.

In my mind my father's name is invariably engraved upon something gold, not only on this plaque but also on all the medals and other honorary insignia that, continuously atinkle on his gold watch chain, testified wherever he went to his brilliant success. He had earned so much gold—money, that is—in the three years since setting up practice that the mental association is inevitable, like "sweet" with "sugar" or "sour" with "lemon" or "cold" with my image of his glittering and metallic personality. He had never known a failure. One year after leaving University Hospital, where he had served his internship and residency in cardiology, he had been able to pay back Grandpa Thomas the fifteen thousand dollars he had borrowed from him to acquire his M.D. and at the same time feed, house, and clothe my mother, brother, and me. That he had "broken" Grandma Thomas's heart by giving up his idea of becoming a missionary to the Chinese had been forgotten in the universal appreciation of his success. The few occasions in his lifetime when he spoke to me of anything other than his success are all, I think, recorded in this memoir. Success went to my mother's head too. I can still hear her boasting about him.

On the doorknob of his new door there hung a second plaque, also gold but not so big, that said, "Walk In Without Ringing." My aunt and I did so. And I was amazed. My old, my original, my only home no longer existed. All of it had been changed by a decorator—by, I found out later, Miss Kopestonsky, who possessed artistic inclinations. Gone was the bowerlike darkness of the staircase where I used to spy on my father's patients as they arrived or walked to the lavatory to undress or urinate in a bottle. Gone were the walls, even, that once separated the stairs from the hall. Gone, too, were the light fixtures hung so high up on the ceiling. Everything I remembered was gone, replaced in every instance either by emptiness or by something gold. *Gold*. I do not mean to harp on the subject as my father so embarrassingly did, as even my mother did. But the omnipresence of gold in the upholstery, the carpets, the very color of the walls, boasted without a qualm of my father's wealth. It bragged of the country boy who had made good.

On entering the golden place in tandem with my aunt, I found no difficulty in putting up with the change, once I took it in. As I paraded through the waiting room, crowded by elderly people with furtive faces, I wondered if they recognized me as the important personage I was, namely my father's elder son, clad in the golden cloth of his name: Charles Thomas, Junior.

Unaware that my father kept office hours just as long as there was someone in the waiting room, my aunt said, "Well, we are either awfully early or awfully late for dinner," and the pair of us ascended the stairs, before the whitish eyes of the sick people, in a kind of royal procession.

The second floor had been changed also. At its rear, where my father and mother used to have their bedroom, whose keyhole had been one of my earliest spying and listening posts (I had sensed trouble brewing even then), there was now a dining room occupied by an extremely long, gold-tinted table. Chairs with seats and backs of petit point, worked in gold wool, were pulled up to it as though for a banquet, although only four places were actually laid at its far end. The bathroom had become the kitchen. And at the front of the floor, where several rooms once existed, including my own, there was now but one—a vast chamber, high, the full width of the house and half its length. Its walls were hung with strangely dolorous landscapes of brown trees, orange skies, and shadowy, blue-hided cows.

36

Its furnishings, round and plush, were likewise unfamiliar. As I gazed at them, at the transformation of my origins, a sense of disenchantment pervaded me.

The feeling did not surprise me. Disenchantment was the fundamental law of my relationship with my father. Thus, as I entered the room, I was ready for it.

Despite everything Aunt Margaret had said against Miss Kopestonsky, I expected the woman who had captured my father to be an improvement over my mother—prettier, sweeter, kinder, maybe even sadder. Not at all. The stranger who was present to greet us turned out to be a very tall woman with giraffe legs who stood up and up and up until her freshly marceled brown hair seemed to brush the ceiling like our Christmas tree. Glancing at me, her yellow eyes stared down with the most untranslatable gleams: I understood that glance no better than I did the sheen of the ornaments on our tree. Although her mouth, broad and palely pomaded, opened in what evidently was intended as a smile of welcome, they actually made a show of teeth at me—the longest, sharpest, most jagged teeth I had ever seen. I knew her at once: my stepmother-to-be. There was no need for me to hear her name fluttering like a flag of momentary truce from my aunt's skillfully dissimulating lips:

"Nina Kopestonsky!"

"Margaret Thomas!"

Their voices echoed in the huge room while they contemplated each other. Considering their previous closeness (if that is the correct word for their rivalry for the affections of the rich and philanthropic Jean Phillips), each had to take an instant to clear away bad, if not bitter, memories of the other before beginning a new relationship in another country in a situation anticipated by neither. Their gazes coruscated with the curiosity and simultaneous disdain of erstwhile friends. Then, with a flip of white kid, my aunt indicated me: "And this is Charlie J."

"I could have guessed," Miss Kopestonsky said. "He favors Charles."

Since I hated Miss Kopestonsky not only with my own feelings but with my poor mother's too, I ignored her ungainly hand, which she offered me so unenthusiastically, and said to her, "You look like a vampire!"

My aunt was shocked, embarrassed, annoyed. "Charlie J!" she cried. "Miss Kopestonsky—Nina—is probably my second-best friend in the world!"

"I don't care. She looks like a vampire to me."

My aunt handled this little crisis with cosmopolitan deftness. Telling me to take off my coat and galoshes and sit in the big gold-upholstered chair on the other side of the room, she led Miss Kopestonsky to a love seat, also upholstered in gold, and joined her, her right arm at rest along the darkly burnished curve of its back so that, in the general glow of a nearby lamp, they formed a pair of silhouettes turned face to face—like a pastel entitled "The Gossips." Gossip was only the least of what took place, however. As a fact I will never forget, it being the first deliberate act of treachery I ever witnessed, my aunt leaned over and lightly kissed Miss Kopestonsky's thin and now red-mottling cheek: "It's good to see you again, Nina."

Miss Kopestonsky said nothing in reply. She kept one dog-brown eye upon me as if she dreaded what I might say next. And I was studying her. Unprepossessing as she was, she dressed unusually well; this was, no doubt, the *je ne sais quoi* my aunt had mentioned to my mother. At this original meeting of ours, she wore a printed taffeta—as I was to discover, she never, winter or summer, wore any other material—and whenever she moved, which she did continuously out of nervousness or downright fear, she rustled, her body one long unbroken sigh.

I said nothing. I was so angry at Miss Kopestonsky's presence in my father's house of gold that I am able to recall very little about that occasion except my emotions. She and my aunt did, I believe, speak of Jean Phillips, of my aunt's work, of Paris, and of Indianapolis where—my aunt came right out and asked—Miss Kopestonsky admitted having spent the holidays. My memory of that half-hour is undoubtedly unreliable, for if Miss Kopestonsky had really and truly been plain and common, how could she have possessed such charm for my father?

Other than my aunt's Judas kiss and my telling Miss Kopestonsky she looked like a vampire, I recall with clarity only one more incident from our visit.

That took place when my aunt interrupted their talk, which was subdued and discreet to the point, I now realize, of wariness, and reached for Miss Kopestonsky's left hand, took hold of it and raised it to her eyes as if she were my father diagnosing a sore knuckle, and said, "You're still wearing it!" She was gazing at Miss Kopestonsky's ring.

Possibly because Miss Kopestonsky had already been unnerved by my insult and my unrelenting glower from the chair across the room, possibly for subtler reasons I have not divined in the relationship between her and my aunt, she jerked her hand back into the shadows that the lamp cast along with its chalky light. Then she thrust the same hand straight out in front of her in a gesture I had seen before when my mother's friends were displaying engagement or wedding rings. Set off by that boastful pose, meeting the light, outlined against the darkness, the ring glittered like fire. It was enormous. Its stones were multicolored, red, green, blue, yellow. Their snakelike flashings made me shudder. Remembering them, I shudder still.

Touching the ring, my aunt was clearly fascinated. "I never expected to see it again," she said. She grew so thoughtful over its cold radiance that Miss Kopestonsky drew it and her hand back as deep into shadow as she could.

Engrossed as I was by my aunt's dealings with Miss Kopestonsky, I can remember clearly my father's arrival from his office downstairs, the electric lights being turned on, the room suddenly brilliant. His hand moved across the back of my head, as transient as a draft of February air. His hands were pink-palmed, stub-fingered, and short-nailed. I heard the jingle of gold, honor, and success on his watch chain. He was wearing his white doctor's jacket with tongue depressors protruding from the breast pocket and a serpentine black stethoscope winding about his neck. The odor of his being was as pronounced as my aunt's, something that I confuse in memory with ether. As usual, he hurried us in to dinner so he could pick up the telephone that was at his place and talk to patients:

"Hello? This is Charles Thomas. You called during office hours. What can I do for you?"

He would listen to patients with a grave attention he never paid my mother, brother, or me. Then, depending on their complaints, he would prescribe bed-rest, aspirin, increased intake of liquids, an enema, or an appointment to consult him in his office. He would promise to make a dozen house calls that very night. While he was on the phone, he ate. If this had not been his lifelong habit, I would say he made every effort to avoid the rest of us, not only me and my aunt, whom he had not seen in several years, but even Miss Kopestonsky. Maybe it is only my sense of the drama that was just beginning that leads me to make such a statement. All I can relate with certainty is that, when dinner was over, he stood up and said that if we did not mind waiting while he read some electrocardiograms he would be glad to run me and my aunt home in his car.

In the half-hour-or-so's wait between dinner and our departure, my aunt finished up the business of the ring.

She and Miss Kopestonsky once again took places on the love seat in the living room. Full of dinner, which had been excessively rich, and amazed, no doubt, by my father's lack of interest in them, the two women said nothing. Then Aunt Margaret leaned over a second time and touched the ring on her old friend's finger. "I need it, Nina," she said. "After all, it really is mine. I'm sure Charles will buy you a much bigger and prettier one." Whereupon, with the blandness of a mechanic going about his job, she twisted the irradiating ring off Miss Kopestonsky's peculiarly passive hand and slipped it onto her own. My most vivid memory of that evening is of Miss Kopestonsky extending her arm, as she had done before, and gazing at her bare hand, its five fingers creased and discolored like a bunch of parsnips.

I remember something else from that visit. When my father drove us home, Miss Kopestonsky accompanied us. She was to be dropped off first at the house in North Philadelphia where, in spite of her obvious position in my father's life, she still kept an apartment. We drove there via the dark, straight, snow-piled avenues of row houses, all of us silent, my aunt fondling the ring on her finger, my father wiping fog off the windshield with his customary impatience. When the car stopped in front of a house whose windows, all lightless, appeared to be made of black ice, as shiny as patent leather, Miss Kopestonsky, saying nothing, climbed out of the front seat. As she did so, something happened—my father did something that elicited from her tight-set mouth a scream of laughter as loud and silly as that of any girl of my age. I can still see it—that yipe—forming in an elongated balloon as from the lips of a character in the funny papers. It was as odd to see as to hear. It outraged my aunt. She stood up in the back seat, where she and I had been relegated by Miss Kopestonsky's bland assumption of the front one. She grabbed the door that was hanging open as wide as my mouth and slammed it shut, saying, "Drive on, Charles." Then, when he instantly obeyed, she added with evangelical severity, "Really, Charles. In front of your own son. In front of a little boy. I can never forgive you that." Then she fell back onto the seat beside me.

Only now, years later, do I realize that as Miss Kopestonsky climbed out of the car my father must have pinched her rear end. In those days I pondered his gesture and her reaction to it (which I recognize now as a shriek of pride) without any precise comprehension. Thus, next day, when I told my mother he had made love to Miss Kopestonsky, I was not lying, since that was what I believed. And possibly my father believed the same.

Worn out by the happenings of that evening, I was unable to man my listening post on the back stairs after my father dropped my aunt and me at the foot of our still-snowy driveway. I therefore cannot report what my aunt told my mother about our visit or what my mother begged to know.

I can, though, reprint my aunt's account of the evening from a letter she wrote, doubtless before the night was out, to Jean Phillips:

My dearest Jean,

At long last I have found the time from my typewriter to get to town and have a little reunion with Charles, who, in case you don't remember, is my baby brother and my darling dear. I am happy to report that he has turned out to be Everything I ever dreamed. He is now The Most Successful Doctor in Philadelphia. His waiting room is as crowded as the banks of the Ganges. He is the Hardest Worker I ever met, including Yours Truly. Yes, he is like me, always anxious to measure up, to come out on top. But, as I always said to you, WHERE would the world BE if *someone* didn't CARE? Chas. does care, and I am very very very proud of him.

You will never guess in a trillion years, though, whom I ran into at his office. NINA KOPESTONSKY! Our bad penny has turned up here. Leg all better. Her whole being much improved, including spiritually. Time and The Wonder of His Works have improved the eminently improvable. She was nice (in her way) to me. She spoke with *much interest* of you and asked, if I ever (ha!)

43

wrote to you, to pass on her best regards. So here they are, for what they are worth!

What about YOURSELF? Why don't you WRITE? Would love to hear.

As ever,
M.

P.S. Another pamphlet will go off to you tomorrow.

I found her letters stuffed at random in the bottoms of her steamer-trunks where my mother must have packed them, together with the rest of her belongings, after my father led her out of our house forever. She did not mail them, I suppose, because she must have despaired of Jean Phillips ever answering them. Only her pamphlets apparently were welcome.

There exists another letter, obviously written the next day. Opening again with "My dearest Jean," it reads:

In my note of last night I did not tell you the whole truth. My conscience hurts me that I didn't. It was simple cowardice on my part.

The fact is, when I write you that N.K. had been nice to me, I didn't tell you just how nice. She gave me the ring. Yes, the DEAREST ring you gave her and about which I stirred up such a silly foolish hornet's nest. Whether it was guilt or what that impelled her, I do not know. But, having heard from me about my current impecuniousness, she just slipped it off her finger and gave it to me, saying, "Here, Margaret, sell it and put the money to good use for the furtherance of the work!" Can you *believe* it?

There is no reason for you to be hurt by her making

44

a gift of the ring to me. After all, you did buy it originally for me. You said you did.

I told her about your GREAT FINANCIAL RETRENCHMENT. How you had your precious Percherons put to sleep rather than see them in someone else's possession. How few pamphlets you feel you can publish now. I keep sending them to you, by the way, just because HE keeps on dictating to me and because someday you might find A Way. I pray so every day.

As ever,
M.

Next day and the day after, I noticed that Aunt Margaret was not wearing Miss Kopestonsky's ring.

I asked her about it. Giving me a look as if to ascertain that I was not a thief bent on filching it from her, she took a small brass key out of her purse, opened the topmost drawer of her dresser, removed an ordinary strong box, tin painted green, and unlocked it before my eyes. It contained nothing but the ring. Hoisting me onto her bony lap, she showed it to me close up. "You see?" she said. "This is what is called a 'dearest' ring because if you take the first letter of the name of each of the stones it spells the word 'dearest.' See? D for diamond, E for emerald, A for amethyst, R for ruby, E for emerald again, S for sapphire, and T for topaz."

I said it must have cost an awful lot of money.

"And an awful lot of pain," she said. Whereupon she put it back inside the box, locked it, and returned the box to the dresser drawer and the key to her purse. Her way of handling the ring, so careful, so proud, made me think of my father and all his boastings. I wondered if he had not stored his success in his mind, as she had the "dearest" ring in the box.

My mother also had my father on her mind. In the following days there was no letup in her white-lipped, silver-eyed quizzing of me: "You can tell Mother everything, dear. How is your daddy? Does he look well? Has he put on weight? Did he say anything about me?"

"No."

"No—what?"

"He didn't say anything about you."

"He didn't take you aside when your Aunt Margaret was out of the room and just whisper into your ear to find out how I was?"

"She was never out of the room."

My cruel adherence to the facts infuriated her. She seldom lost her temper, and it was extremely interesting to me to observe how the pink of her eyelids deepened into maroon when my blunt answers provoked her, how her eyes flashed with rage and injury simultaneously, how her lips turned as white as if once again she had been assuaging her grief with box after box of marshmallows. Her anger was so unfamiliar to me that I studied her reaction several times before admitting that in addition to Aunt Margaret and myself someone else had been present throughout the evening.

"Who? Tell Mother, dear. You can tell her everything."

"A tall lady like a giraffe with big teeth."

"A Miss Kopestonsky?"

"Yes, and she hugged Aunt Margaret and talked to her for a long time and then gave her a big ring."

46

"Miss Kopestonky hugged your aunt?"

"No, I guess it was the other way around."

"Your aunt hugged her?"

"Yes, and then when we were driving home Daddy made love to her."

"Made love to her?"

"He reached out and did something bad to her when she was getting out of the car."

"And what did your Aunt Margaret do?"

"She stood up in the back seat and got mad."

I was cruel to my mother for several complicated reasons, chiefly because I blamed her for my father's abandonment of us. It never occurred to me that the fault might be his—that he might actually prefer an odd and strained entanglement such as he was having with the ugly Miss Kopestonsky to the direct, if not exactly simple, life he had led with my mother, so charming when she was not down in the dumps. Her prettiness was composed of warm whites, rosy pinks, the delicate blues or greens or grays of her changing eyes, a youthful palette that I, with my stubborn responses to her questions, helped to spoil. . . .

When her anger showed scarlet and dead-white upon her face, which had exceptionally regular features, she would grow silent and sit motionless, seeming to think and think. A little rash—for the remainder of her life the visible sign of her never-ending passion for my father—would come and go, now on her throat, now on one cheek, now on the other, sometimes on her forehead, sometimes—like a beauty patch—next to her upper lip, and sometimes in the wishbone angle between the top of her nose and her brow, never becoming the blemish she imagined it to be.

47

She tried numberless cures for it—ointments, powders, pills, and diets, including a daily drop of arsenic in a tumbler of water. Nothing removed it. Nothing could remove it. My mother's rash was a sign of the violence concealed within her meekness, the Southern rebelliousness under the Southern femininity to which she had been raised.

One day, while I was at school and Aunt Margaret was laboring at her typewriter, the violence broke loose. Somehow, probably through acquaintances of my aunt's who were also friends of Miss Kopestonsky's, Mother got in touch with Nina Kopestonsky at her apartment in North Philadelphia. She spoke to Miss Kopestonsky on the phone. She told her she was a wicked woman. An adulteress. A harlot. She said that on account of what she had done she —Miss Kopestonsky—was going to burn in hellfire for eternity. (I know this to be a fact because she reported it to Aunt Margaret after dinner when I was supposed to be upstairs in bed.)

Nor did Mother leave it at that. She managed to get in touch with the fundamentalist sect, the Lord's Something-or-other, that had sponsored Miss Kopestonsky's work in Indianapolis and eventually established her connection with Jean Phillips abroad. My mother informed one of its chief officials of Miss Kopestonsky's sexual depredations. That was the roundabout way she put it: "Miss Kopestonsky's sexual depredations." She also phoned Miss Kopestonsky's landlady at that lightless row house in North Philadelphia and denounced her profligacy to her.

My aunt was aghast: "You didn't, Star! Did you?"

"I did. I had to."

The result of all this vengeance turned out to be exactly

the opposite of what my mother desired. True, the official of the fundamentalist sect disposed of Miss Kopestonsky's services, whatever they may have been, without explanation. Her landlady evicted her. So without a cent to her name or so much as a ring to carry to a pawnshop, Miss Kopestonsky turned straight to my father. From that day on, she lived with him openly.

It was not long before I myself was drawn into this adult mess. One day I came home from school and saw on my mother's features the telltale rash, half a dozen pinkish welts that clung like parasites to her right temple.

In solemn tone she said, "Your daddy's going to pick you up at seven o'clock to make calls with him tonight."

Guessing that his invitation had something to do with Miss Kopestonsky, something angry, something unpleasant, I said I had too much homework to do.

"Your daddy wants you to make calls with him," my mother said, "and you'll go, young man."

At dinner Aunt Margaret paused in chewing her milk to say, "Maybe Charles would like me to ride along with him and Charlie J."

"He only said Charlie J," said my mother.

The dot of seven o'clock. Mother and I are at the front door. Her face bends down to kiss me, its marshmallow breath slightly sour from the strain of recent days. Her features are wearier than I have ever seen them. They have about them a darkness. Her eyes are blue—and furtive. I understand that she is trying not to see my father, who, having honked the horn twice, has parked his new Stude-

49

baker, glittering like a Venetian barge, at the foot of our driveway.

"Hello, son," he says, and kisses me.

His mouth, always damp-lipped, always tastes of metallic medicine. He pats my knee with a heartiness I know to be false. His back is unusually straight compared to most people's, his neck as stiff as his starched white collar. Although he is seated at the wheel of his new car (all his life he will have new cars—Chryslers, Caddies, Lincolns—that he wears, so to speak, as he does the gold trophies on his watch chain), he does not seem to have his pride today— he is nervous. As we drive off, I place myself beside him alertly.

We do not drive far. We park in front of a high wall. I prepare myself as best I can, stiffening, I imagine, my nonexistent morale. He and I are going to "have a little talk." He is going to lose his temper, after all. Though I do not yet know of my mother's vendetta against Miss Kopestonsky, I have surmised—I have deduced as astutely as an astronomer—its presence or that of something like it.

Pretending to be calm, I turn my face from him and study the high wall. It is of cream-colored stucco, all smeary on purpose. It is roofed with red tiles as if it were a long narrow house. A tree stretches one bony branch over the wall. Sparrows sit on the branch like old brown leaves. The sidewalk is a puddle of mud. I decide that, no matter what happens, I will not cry, I will not give him the satisfaction. . . .

Then he picks up the doctor's bag that sits between us on the seat (it is black and bears in gold the initials "C.T.")

and says, "Come with me, son," and I get out and follow him across the mud of the sidewalk into an opening in the wall and walk with him up a black driveway to a Spanish-looking house where a door made of black, iron curlicues opens before he can ring the bell. We wipe our feet. We cross a hall. We climb a flight of stairs at the heels of an old woman in a wool bathrobe who has murmured something to him that I am too mystified to understand. Another door, a wooden one, opens. We are in a bedroom where I see nothing but a bed, and in the bed an old man so huge that he and the sheet that covers him are spilling, it seems to me, over its sagging edge. The old woman's hand, like one of my teachers', firmly detains me at the doorway. My father, however, walks on and lifts the sheet off the old man and bares his stomach. It is bigger than a woman's when she is going to have a baby. It is naked. It has white hairs on it. And a navel. I think of a giant orange that has rotted. It is very interesting to see.

My father's hand comes into view. It holds a large needle with a white-striped bottle, or something like a bottle, only longer, on the end of it. His hand pushes the needle into the rotten orange just to the right of the navel and the white hairs. The old man says nothing. He is merely an old man's head. He has no connection with the orange. . . .

Meanwhile, the bottle at the end of the needle is filling up with a thick and yellowish-green liquid. When the bottle is almost full, my father takes the needle out of the orange and squirts its contents into a dishpan underneath the bed. I see the liquid is more yellow than green. And frothy.

Again the needle pierces the orange and the bottle fills up and the liquid is emptied into the dishpan. The pan is going to overflow. The orange, I see, is shrinking.

Finally the orange disappears altogether and instead there is an old man's stomach, rubbery, loose-skinned, pink. My father's hand swabs it with a wad of cotton and then bandages it with adhesive tape. The old man's head has now become part of his body, as small as my own, and for some reason embarrassing for me to see.

Suddenly I realize that all this time my father has been talking to the old man. I have not heard a word until he has said, "Come on, son," and down we go with the old woman to the wrought-iron door and it opens and out we walk into an early spring twilight that is like a green leaf all wet with rain.

Never having been supplied an explanation of my father's purpose in showing me this awful, if fascinating, operation, I can merely speculate while I recall it. Did he want me to see with my own eyes his prowess as a physician? Did he want me to value him for that, if for nothing else? Did he want to punish me with the horror of such a long, drawn-out sight? Did he want to befuddle my mind with it before he told me what he was about to tell me? I am unable to say.

Twilight darkens now that we are out-of-doors again. The deep blue and purple clouds are piled like an incredible season's bloom in the forks and crotches of the black and still-budless trees of the suburbs.

We do not drive far. We park. This time, although I turn my face, there is no wall to stare at. There is no house in sight. I see a field of tan grass turning white under a swell of the March evening's pale breeze. A crow flies up. It croaks. And disappears. The sky grows darker, and yet there is a white light shining somewhere. I am able to make out my father's face with unusual clarity—the pallor edged by the blue of his close shave, the handsomeness of his Thomas profile, so like Aunt Margaret's, and the exact lines of a new haircut. The crow caws again. Several of them are marauding the waves of the vacant field. . . .

Then I look at my father again and am startled. He has turned to me. Inasmuch as a grownup can do so (he is five feet eleven inches tall) underneath the horn-colored circle of the steering wheel, he is kneeling. Kneeling to me. And looking at me. His eyes, as black as a crow, seem to want to embrace mine. Before I can look away, I see they are watering. A liquid that shines silver in the twilight appears on his eye-sockets and on his cheeks and on down where the blue stubble sharply starts. My father is crying. *Crying!* My father! His mouth, too, is watering. He is saying something I do not understand. "Son." And his hand is on my knee again, not hearty now, not false.

"Son," he says.

The word is watery, like his eyes, like his mouth, but I understand it now.

At this point he falters, stops, cannot go any further. "Son," he says again. But that is all.

I want to help him. I want to say, "What?" But I am too afraid of him.

In my memory it is an occasion identical with the time, many years later, when Grandpa Thomas died and his ashes lay in a package no bigger than a small box of cereal and they were wrapped in plain white paper tied by plain

53

white string. My father, holding the box in his lap, started to weep, and I, the only other passenger in the undertaker's limousine, was either unable or unwilling to reach out a hand to comfort him.

As I stare at my father's eyes and mouth, he finds the words he has evidently planned to say to me all along.

Son. Can you forgive me? I did not want things to turn out the way they have. I ought to have stayed with the Church as Mama wanted. Your mother and I ought to have gone to China and been missionaries the way we planned. I don't deserve the success I have had. Or the money. Oh, son. You know in your heart that all your dad has ever really wanted was for you boys and your mother to be happy. . . .

I am unable to place quotation marks around his words, for in my fear of him, and then in my amazement at his apology, I did not hear him accurately.

The episode was so unlike him, so unique in my lifetime's experience of him, that it has remained in my memory as vividly as a painting: the white-topped grass blowing, the crows cawing, his eyes watering, and out of his too-regular mouth coming these unexpected regrets, which, it is clear to me, were guilts as painful as the flames of hellfire to which my mother had consigned Miss Kopestonsky instead of him.

The next memorable event took place not long afterward, during the first weeks of April.

I came down with a cold. I grew so sick, with such a high temperature, that I was put to bed. The weather of my body stayed wintry while the out-of-doors turned mild.

My mother looked after me. As expert and thoughtful a nurse as she was a cook and housekeeper, she made pots of chicken soup for me, she prepared cup-custards, my favorite dessert. Once a day, usually in the middle of the lengthy afternoon, she would bring an apple to my bed and, scraping its pale-green meat out of the red rind with one of her sterling-silver Sunday dinner knives, would feed me that chill and acrid treat, spilling it now and then because of a subtle tremor in her hand, which was as skilled as a milkmaid's. Afterward, she would read aloud the best scenes from *Treasure Island*, always beginning with Jim hiding in the apple barrel on deck. In her voice I overheard her continuing agitation. She had ceased speaking of it to me directly. And I was growing used to it. It seemed as much a part of her nature as the volatile rash on her otherwise transparent complexion.

The event that I am relating was clearly the result of this restrained unhappiness within her. One day she decided I needed some nose drops. She went to the medicine cabinet downstairs in her own bathroom and came back with a small brown glass bottle from which she unscrewed and filled a red rubber dropper. Saying, "Now breathe in, dear," she squirted its contents high and stinging into my clogged sinuses.

"It tastes funny," I said.

Whereupon she glanced at the bottle, dropped it to the floor, where it broke, and ran out of the room. She ran down the stairs, screaming all the way, "My God! My God! I've poisoned my own child!"

Instead of nose drops, she had given me some of the arsenic that she took for her rash.

I could hear her running through the house like a madwoman, repeating her terrifying assertion.

My aunt stayed calm. Emerging in her usual dishevelment from her room, she telephoned my father and asked him what should be done for a case of arsenic poisoning.

He advised milk, as many quarts of it as could be poured down my gullet.

My aunt collected as much milk from our refrigerator as it contained—there were three quart bottles, I remember, one half-full—and sent my mother to the neighbors to fetch more. Then she came to my bedside and proceeded with reassuring calm and efficiency to feed me glass after glass. My mother arrived with several more quarts.

The dose of arsenic, quite minuscule in spite of all the alarm, did me no harm. I recall no pain at all other than the anticipation and pity of my premature demise.

Although, as things turned out, I was not myself the victim of the mishap, my mother was. Horrified at her carelessness, exhausted by the emotions of the past months, certain at last of Miss Kopestonsky's ascendancy in my father's heart, she collapsed. She had to be put to bed. As a matter of fact, my brother, supposedly too young to be aware of what was happening in our family, also fell ill with a cold. Thus Aunt Margaret, whose talents extended "no further," as one of her unsent letters to Jean Phillips frankly states, "than the lectern and the typewriter," was left in charge of a houseful of sick children.

Being the first to take to bed, I was the first to get out. One night I was permitted to go downstairs for supper. My aunt and I ate at the kitchen table. When we finished, she prepared trays for my fellow invalids upstairs.

56

"I will be back in a minute," she said. "Go into the den and lie down on the sofa."

Having discovered from necessity that she was capable of heating a can of soup, of scrambling or poaching an egg, of making milktoast, my aunt seemed to enjoy exercising her novel authority in our household. In fact, she was apt to become bossy, keeping us on the strictest of schedules, rousing my mother from one of her deathlike sleeps, for instance, in order to ply her with sedatives, requiring me to listen to passages not from *Treasure Island* but from the Bible, usually the twenty-third psalm and John 3:16.

While she was tending the others, I was likely to suffer pangs of that sense of exile that had been plaguing me since our move to the suburbs. On this particular night, when she was upstairs spoon-feeding my mother and brother in their separate rooms, I went as she suggested to the den. Despite a blue-flamed fire burning in the grate, the room seemed desolate. The darkness of early evening seemed to isolate me, to bury me out of reach of all communication and rescue. The darkness covered the many-paned windows like a blizzard. There was no sound. Even the fire flickered as noiselessly as though it were an image in a nightmare, irrationally meaningful. The oddly slow motions of the flames, as I watched them, reminded me, perhaps because they resembled the taffeta of Miss Kopestonsky's clothing, of my father and of her who had taken possession of him. Ugly Miss Kopestonsky. So tall. So ill at ease. So silly when my father had pinched her backside. I wondered what it looked like, really, back there under her ruffles and sashes, like a pillow pinned for some unknown reason to the base of her spine. . . . As I entertained these thoughts, I suffered for the first time what I can honestly describe only as one of my "fits." I shook all over. My hands shook. So did my arms, my shoulders, my neck, my head, my very eyes, all of me.

Of this instant all I can recall with any accuracy is Aunt Margaret's sudden reappearance. She leaned in the doorway, electric light to her back, and, having peered into the firelit darkness, suddenly spoke my name: "Charlie J!" She set down what she was carrying, probably the trays laden with my mother's and brother's dirty dishes, and came directly and purposefully, lacking all emotion, to the sofa where I was writhing. She sat down. She raised me into her arms. She lifted me onto her lap. She held me as if I were a mere baby, rocking me, her mouth warm against my ear. She said to me the beautiful, precise, and caressing words she had uttered once before: "Be still. Be still. Be still." She repeated them until, after I do not know how long, perhaps an hour, possibly a single minute, my fit ended, and I lay watching the fire, so blue, so embracing, so warm.

"My darling," she said, "you might as well learn that life is not easy. It isn't supposed to be. Not even for children. That's not how our Lord planned it. But let Aunt Margaret tell you a secret, will you? Will you? Be still. Be as still as if it were always the end of the day, the end of winter. Ask nothing. Expect nothing. Just be still. Like a flower. Like a blade of common old Johnson grass. Do you hear your aunt? Let life happen to you and try to be still, no matter what it brings, the best or the worst or— what is maybe the hardest of all—neither anything very good or very bad. Someday you will understand what I am saying, Charlie J. Accept. Just accept. It is the best blessedness He has given us—stillness. Listen. Do you hear it? The stillness of the flower seeds in the ground? Find your stillness, my darling, and abide by it forever. Listen to your Aunt Margaret, dear. She has been clear around the world seven times, and she, I assure you, knows."

I heard her. I heard, and for the first time in many months I came to rest—my body, my nerves, my mind. The fire of my anguish, both simple and complex, burned out as surely as the flames in the grate, flickering more and more distantly, like the blue wings of a bird receding or a blue comet fading in the night sky.

CHAPTER

THREE

When my mother's turn came to get out of bed she was so weak, so heavily sedated with phenobarbital, so withdrawn and tonguetied, that I, watching, wondered if she also had taken one of Aunt Margaret's lessons in stillness.

Because it was spring, she began to pass the day in our garden in back of the house and the garage. On account of my father's decision not to move with us to the suburbs, which apparently had been as much a surprise to her as it had been to me, she had not planted the garden during the autumn as she had planned to. It was a big garden, almost half an acre. Flagstone paths led through thickets of rho-dodendron to a concrete birdbath where the cardinals, plashing fountains of scarlet, played all day long.

In those first yellow-tinted days of the new season, the garden was beautiful. For my mother, who loved flowers and all things green, it ought to have been a pleasure and continuous surprise. She regarded it as neither. Insofar as I—spying from the corner pane of my third-floor window —could tell, she did not even look at it. She merely plumped herself down in the middle of it, paler than the squills, the narcissus, or the whitest daffodils, her eyes and the skin beneath them darker than the violets, which appeared in astonishing abundance, the water on her cheek as predict-able as the morning dew on the grass. In the unreliable warmth of April and the inescapable alternating dapple of shadow cast by the big oak, the pair of maples, and the apple trees just beginning to come into leaf, she let her sorrow bloom.

Just as my mother neither saw nor admired her garden, she neither worked nor cut it. A green-handled trowel, new, lay on the weedy ground. So did a pair of clippers, also new. My mother merely went on sitting. Whether it was a dry day or a damp one, she often lay down at full length, arms and legs askew, her hair outspread, like the victim of a bolt of lightning. Once she so immersed herself in the rapidly rising and thickening green that I was unable to locate her —and was scared. Reminding myself of the necessity of re-maining calm, I went downstairs to the dresser in her bed-room, opened its sachet-scented top drawer full of white gloves and lace-edged handkerchiefs, and found her opera glasses, mother-of-pearl and gold, which had been the gift of my father's very first grateful patient. I carried them back upstairs and used them to find her. What I actually saw were the muddy toes of her shoes underneath the red-streaked stems of some already fat-budded peonies. . . .

This loss of my mother, which I took with more fright than I dared admit to myself, happened quite late on the afternoon of a marine-toned day when the greenery and the flowers were blowing as slowly as if they were under water. I was still watching, studying through the opera glasses my mother's plain brown shoes as if they were clues to a mystery, when Aunt Margaret, leaving her room earlier than usual, strolled to the garden. Listening intently, I heard her say to my mother, "I believe I will go into town and have a little chat with Charles. Do you mind if I cut some flowers?"

My mother sat up dazedly, her glance as awry as the straw hat on her head, and said, "Take all you want, Margaret. The garden needs a good thinning anyhow."

Under my magnified scrutiny, my aunt picked a bouquet of grape hyacinths, blue squills, and blue pansies. My mother did not notice its prettiness, so French, so unexpectedly feminine. If I did not guess that it was destined for Miss Kopestonsky, I feel sure I knew it had something to do with my aunt's project of bringing my father back to us. Later, as I watched my aunt climb into the back seat of a Yellow Cab, the audacity of her project frightened me. No one I knew had ever defied my father and gotten away with it. My mother had tried. As I understood the situation, his abandonment of us was our punishment for her desire to live in the country.

As soon as Aunt Margaret was driven away, I decided, out of anxiety, to join my mother in the garden.

The garden, even so early in the spring, was taller than

63

I partly because as it extended back from the house it was terraced in higher and higher levels, partly because my mother had permitted it to grow so wild. Iris, still green and as tightly furled as umbrellas, poked up straight. Lavender lilacs drooped overhead. Squills and grape hyacinths fringed the unmown rectangles of grass. Because of the late hour the light was dim. Haze was descending. Pushing aside the brown stems of a clump of coral bells, I came upon my mother stretched out exactly as she had been earlier, limbs sprawled, hair spread, hat atilt on the back of her thought-filled motionless head. I was amazed and annoyed by her relaxation at the very moment when Aunt Margaret was bringing danger down on us again. I asked when we were going to eat.

"Eat?" she said, sitting up and making a preposterous pretense of shading her wet eyes against the waning light.

"It's after seven," I said.

"It is?"

"I'm hungry."

"Mother will be in and fix you something in a minute."

"I hope we have a good supper."

"Hasn't your Aunt Margaret been giving you nice hot meals, honey?"

"She's gone," I said.

But there was no rousing her to the danger that I feared. I was astounded by her ignorance of it. As I stood there hoping to jolt her out of her melancholy, her face broke out again, the little rash materializing right before my worried eyes. Her left cheek looked as if a peony or rose had shed its palest petals there.

The single result of my oblique warning was that next

day Mother hired a maid to do the cooking, a black girl, eighteen-years-old, whose name was Patience.

The effect of my aunt's first skirmish with Miss Kopestonsky? Next morning I saw nothing on her face that told me. When my mother asked if my father had been pleased by the flowers, my aunt said, "Why not? Charles has country in his blood too." I deducted from this remark, as brusque as a sergeant's, that, whatever may have happened in town, she had not yet angered him.

I was taken along on her next trip to town. Henceforth, in fact, I was always taken along, probably as an excuse for the frequency of her trips ("A growing boy needs to see his father as often as he can"), probably also at the urging of my mother, so visibly desirous of accompanying us but, weakened by her vegetable meekness and despair, willing to be present by proxy instead.

On our second trip to town our bouquet for Miss Kopestonsky was of daffodils—so many and so yellow, wrapped in wet newspaper, that they looked like a cutting of the day's sunshine. Arranged in a blue-and-white ginger jar by Miss Kopestonsky, who, to my surprise, accepted them with no more suspicion than usual, they dulled the gold tones of my father's apartment where she now lived permanently. She poked the long putty-colored length of her nose into the daffodils' perfectly wrought cups, breathed to the bottom of her lungs, and then breathed out, sighing, "Spring!"

I expected that innocent inhalation to knock her unconscious. It didn't. Instead, she made a pot of tea for Aunt

Margaret and herself and brought me a bottle of orange pop. She was almost relaxed, almost friendly. She looked healthier, less ugly. Her taffeta dress riffled and rustled only slightly. I perceived that she had benefited greatly by my mother's impetuous attempt at vengeance.

The one significant turn of this visit took me by surprise. Seated on the love seat, Aunt Margaret put down her gold-rimmed teacup, reached into her navy-blue purse, and pulled out, without the feminine folderol usually involved in such an action, the "dearest" ring. She handed it to Miss Kopestonsky. "Here, dear," she said. "It's yours. It was given to you even if it was bought for me. I have no right to ask you to donate it to the work."

Miss Kopestonsky wore poise as self-consciously as if it were a new dress. "But I gave it to you, Margaret," she said. "It's yours to do with as you see fit."

My aunt disliked debates, hesitations. Her hand tried forcibly to insert the ring between Miss Kopestonsky's clenched fingers. "I insist, Nina, I absolutely insist!"

"But, Margaret," Miss Kopestonsky finally said, "I don't need it. Not now."

And she raised and opened her left hand to the width of her fingers, displaying for our benefit another ring, this one made entirely of diamonds, big ones that gleamed gold in that room and reflected like shattered mirrors, I thought, the gleams of the daffodils. She did not have to tell us who had given her the ring or why.

My aunt kept the "dearest" ring with a dismay she did not try to conceal, looking, as I recall, yellower than she usually did, yellow-faced and yellow-handed and also yellow-eyed.

"Anyhow," she said in the taxi on our way home from that initial setback "having the ring is like money in the bank."

For her, however, philosophical acceptance of defeat was impossible unless she could be convinced that it was the Will of the Lord. This, of course, was unthinkable. So it was perhaps that very night that she wrote the following undated letter to Jean Phillips:

> Our bad penny has come home with a vengeance. I told you in my last epistle how she tried to entangle Chas. in her snares. It has been exactly like the way she moved in on you and me. She's a real scavenger who feeds on the rot in other people's lives.
>
> Now, thanks to some foolishness on Star's part, she has taken over completely—moved in, bag and baggage. It *breaks* my heart. She is obviously going to be the next Mrs. Charles Thomas.
>
> Oh, my dear, it is all so WRONG! I know He who looks after us from Above will not let it happen. I promise you I will do *Everything In My Power* to make sure it doesn't. . . .

I quote only the pertinent paragraphs of this letter, which otherwise is chatty and intimate, reflecting a need for friendship after her call on her enemy; it records the progress of her work and the improvement in her "patients," by which she presumably meant my mother, brother, and me. Its honest appeal for affection is so straightforward that it causes me to wonder, in today's fashion, about her relationship with Jean Phillips. However lesbian the relationship may have been at heart, it certainly was innocent in both body and mind. Indeed, the words of the letter and of all the rest sound to me like soliloquies, lines addressed to a mirror perhaps, self-dramatizations, like my father's exaggerated confession of guilt to me the day after he punctured the old man's pregnant belly. Probably this helps to explain why she never mailed her letters to the rich woman who is now so prominent, white-haired, and smart on the society pages of the New York papers, where I saw her picture only a week ago.

I date a change in Aunt Margaret from the night Miss Kopestonsky refused the "dearest" ring. From that time on, she certainly regarded herself as the leader of a battle. She acquired a militant, even a military, appearance. Her hair, which hung loose as a cloak until my mother's summons to supper, was now pinned severely close to her head. The ragged slip in which she had done all her typing was replaced by a black dress with brass buttons, similar to a uniform in its cut and worn with the same regularity. Her manner became as authoritative as a general's. She directed our activities—my mother's, brother's, and my own—as if we were troops assigned to her for deployment. Sometimes, for us in varying stages of recuperation from that long and unhappy winter, it was wearying. Aunt Margaret was single-minded to the point of mania.

Thus, in the same way that she must have set out years before to convert to her brand of Christianity all the rest of the world—including, I have been told by someone with a straight face, the Jews—she proceeded to try to stop my father from obtaining a divorce so that he could marry Miss Kopestonsky.

68

Instead of abandoning her campaign of the flowers, which had so far produced nothing but a defeat, my aunt intensified it. The very day after our defeat—the day, that is, after the attempt to give back the "dearest" ring—we took Miss Kopestonsky a bucketful of tulips as red as blood. And thereafter, in a sequence I can no longer remember, we carried her bunches of everything that bloomed in my mother's garden: more tulips; irises of all shades, including a very strange pink one; peonies; sweet Williams; sweet peas; and finally, roses, which flourished prolifically, as earlier the violets had, as fat as peaches.

All these Miss Kopestonsky accepted as her due as victor, jamming them into vases and always bending low to inhale their perfumes, while I, served a bottle of orange pop or cream soda, watched and wondered when their subtle poison—which I imagined to be real, although I think I knew it was actually nothing but my aunt's hatred—would start to work upon her singularly robust system.

In the course of these floral visits of ours, my aunt drank tea and talked. She talked ceaselessly—as if she were at her lectern in front of a thousand gathered heathen. She spoke mostly of Him, Our Lord, The Good Shepherd, The Almighty. Tactlessly, I thought, recalling my mother's vituperous threat, she spoke also of hellfire and damnation, of the eternal tortures held in readiness for those who disobeyed His commands. Yet it was all extraordinarily conversational, apparently mere chitchat between a pair of friends. It sounded no more threatening than the bouquets of flowers looked in their gold vases on the tables, the sills, the gold-hued marble of the mantelpiece.

As far as I could see, Miss Kopestonsky did not suffer

from our calls. She felt no fears. She had no qualms about being Mrs. Charles Thomas-to-be.

Eventually, toward the beginning of June, a good deal later than I anticipated, Miss Kopestonsky fell ill. It was not her bad leg that bothered her. It was not anything that had been seen before in this country. Her case baffled my father, whose fame in those days was chiefly that of a diagnostician. On the theory that in the course of her broad travels she may have been infected by a disease peculiar to other continents, my father put her in the hospital. But her illness defied every test and the skill of every specialist, including those brought in from Baltimore, New York, and Boston.

I daydreamed of telling the truth, namely that Miss Kopestonsky lay in her hospital bed like a corpse because she had inhaled the fumes of too many of our flowers.

Her feeble condition—which in actuality was probably the effect of all the shocks and triumphs she had endured during the past months, plus the guilt of an extremely Christian and neurotic woman—did not evoke in my aunt one iota of pity or sympathy. Nor did it inhibit her purpose. Miss Kopestonsky's situation, in a bed as high as a work table in a dim private room at the end of a long, usually empty, corridor, only invited the gift of more and more flowers. What, after all, did you take to a person sick in bed? Flowers. It struck me that He, with His own mysterious purposes to perform, was encouraging my aunt in hers, helping her miraculously.

And so, rather than a single carefully chosen and well-arranged bouquet, Aunt Margaret and I began lugging in bundles and bunches and buckets and baskets of the hastiest combinations—Canterbury bells with the buttercups that had started to grow wild on our uncut lawn, baby's-breath, light as its name, together with peonies as big and red and wobbly as babies' heads, iris together with oriental poppies whose hairy, oozing green stems my mother would seal by singeing them over a burner on the stove. We took so many flowers that, along with the two dozen American Beauty roses sent daily by my father, they transformed Miss Kopestonsky's private room into an unexpected semblance of my mother's garden. Branches of apple blossoms drooped over the bed. Stuffed vases fenced it. Rose petals and other flotsam rotted on the floor. The sweetly floral odor of the room, commingled with the morbid smells of the hospital, was debilitating and nasty. It seemed to me the stink of weakness. This was, of course, the falsest possible reading of Miss Kopestonsky's predicament. I could not help it. The more she began to look like a bigger, paler, uglier version of my poor mother in her garden, the more I began to sympathize with her.

Our visits were strained. Talk ran short. One day my aunt had to cast around for conversation. Her black brows frowned and squinted. Then she quizzed Miss Kopestonsky about her ailment, about the doctors' latest diagnoses, about what my father had to say. For maybe the hundredth time she warned Miss Kopestonsky against resorting to "the mind doctor," as she called the psychiatrist. She despised the mind doctor.

Miss Kopestonsky, lying there in limp melancholy, supplied the requisite answers but had nothing to say of her own volition.

Again there came a silence.

"I can't warn you too often against the mind doctor,"

my aunt said. "I am quite sure he doesn't believe in God."

"You said that before, Margaret," said Miss Kopestonsky.

My aunt's left eye twitched.

The smell of the flowers grew stronger than ether and put me in an inexplicable panic. For all my faith in my aunt and my desire to see her beat Miss Kopestonsky, I could not stand it—that terribly sweet reek, the tension between the two women, Miss Kopestonsky looking as if she had been killed even before my aunt had wreaked her purpose against her. I begged to be excused to go outside into the fresh air and rain.

"Go ahead," said my aunt with sudden, bitter irritability. "Go ahead and desert the ship!"

When I got outside I was trembling all over.

Having been taken so often to the hospital to visit my father when he was an intern and later chief resident, I was usually thoroughly at home there. The accident ward had been my playroom, and I knew everyone on the staff, from the black orderlies and the pink-faced Irish cooks to the oldest and most eminent physicians; and everyone knew me. Doubtless because of my father's success (years afterward someone told me that the sheer number of his patients had kept the hospital—it was a private one—going during the worst days of the Depression), they made many shows of affection toward me. They would waylay me in the elevator or the corridors, pat my head, and ask about him.

Thus it was through me, invariably laden with one, two, or three bouquets for Miss Kopestonsky, that Aunt Margaret made everybody's acquaintance also.

"I am Charles Thomas's sister," she would say, proffering her mandarin hand.

Then she would proceed—with a pride perhaps not universally admired—to discuss the details of my father's success, the famous or distinguished or merely old Philadelphian names of his clientele, the vast sums of money he earned, the "gorgeousness" (I still remember her unexpected use of that word, which must have been one of Jean Phillips's) of his office. It was in this fashion, which mortified me and my fanatical sense of propriety, that she came to meet Miss Nancy Jones.

Now, Miss Nancy Jones, whose name, with its connotation of youthfulness, belied her thin and remarkably freckled middle age, was an old friend of mine. She was head nurse in charge of Miss Kopestonsky's floor. She wore a cap, unlike the other nurses', that had white, starched wings on either side and was bound across the crown by a black velvet ribbon. Her uniform, never wrinkled, rattled as though it were white tin when she walked. Also I had occasion to detect about her small and efficient person the exotic scent of tobacco. She was the first woman I ever knew who smoked. She was, therefore, a charmer. Much of her charm must have been her talk. A Southerner, from, I believe, Baltimore, she had the Southern woman's desire to please or at least to keep talking no matter what. In that pretty voice of hers, low and soft as a chuckle, she talked at length with my aunt. Afterward, my aunt questioned me about her:

"How long have you known Miss Jones?"

"Ever since I can remember."

"Do you like her?"

"Yes."

"Does your daddy like her?"

"He seems to."

"Does Mother?"

"No."

"Why not?"

"I don't know."

Thinking back on this interrogation, I am dazed at how close Aunt Margaret came to letting me in on her final plan of attack against Miss Kopestonsky. Under the lights that passed through the darkness of the rear of our cab my aunt's face gleamed like a copper mask. I think it possible that she conceived her plan in those few moments of our ride home, although I hesitate to ascribe to her, whom I loved, a plan that proved so diabolical.

Another June day, green again, rainy again, my aunt and I happened to enter the hospital just as Miss Jones was going off duty. She wore a dark blue cape with a shiny red lining. She paused to chat with us, rife with that delicious aroma of cigarette smoke, her brown eyes issuing as much charm as her lips, which, I suddenly noticed in genuine alarm, were painted red, red brighter than the inside of her cape. My aunt, who objected to the use of all cosmetics other than good strong brown soap and water, made no protest against the lipstick, however. Unable to believe she would know a woman who smoked, she did not sniff the tobacco either. She was so pleased to run into Miss Jones that day that she invited her to join us for a cup of tea in the interns' dining room, where, as my father's kin, she and I were made more welcome than in any restaurant.

74

Miss Jones refused. My aunt pressed her. Miss Jones gave in reluctantly.

At this hour—we had come to town earlier than usual—the dining room was empty except for the dietitian, another old friend of mine, an Irish woman named Mary, who seemed to enjoy making a fuss over my aunt and me. Mary always had some tidbit for me: a cookie, a banana, a piece of roast beef very well done with no fat on it. She and I had fun.

My aunt and Miss Jones drank their tea, several cups of it, and discussed Miss Kopestonsky. Miss Jones's opinion of "that strange case," which was how she lispingly referred to her patient, turned out to be that Miss Kopestonsky required the services of a psychiatrist.

Overhearing this heretical statement, I abruptly turned my attention from Mary to my aunt.

Instead of launching into her familiar tirade against the "mind doctor," my aunt allowed the recommendation to pass as unchallenged as the red on Miss Jones's lips or the mind-tingling perfume of her cigarettes.

I wondered why Aunt Margaret exempted Miss Jones from her high standards of conduct.

When belatedly, with our bouquets wilting, but still at an earlier hour than usual, we reached Miss Kopestonsky's room, we found my father there. Wearing his white jacket like a royal robe, his stethoscope like a chain of office, he was peculiarly affable. This mood of his—which I had never before witnessed—was not pleasure in meeting up with my aunt and me but the fact, which he immediately reported to us, that one of the wealthiest men from one of the oldest families in Philadelphia had that morning become his patient: "Mr. Gouverneur Smuggins!" The antique name clinked like one more honorary medal, one more solid gold coin, upon his watch chain. Because of his mood, and because my aunt was also in fine fettle, and because Miss Kopestonsky was neither blue nor whiny, our visit that day was surprisingly satisfying.

My aunt adjusted the timing of all our future visits so that the pleasure might be repeated. It invariably was. It began always with three-quarters of an hour of tea-drinking with Miss Jones. It ended with this glimpse of my father, whose habit it was to call on Miss Kopestonsky before setting out on his rounds of the private and semi-private rooms and the wards.

After we said good-by to Miss Kopestonsky, my father would accompany us down the corridor. He demonstrated great pride in Aunt Margaret, bragging to the white-jacketed crowd who trailed along with him of her vast acquaintanceship overseas, mispronouncing the names of countesses and celebrities, yet impressing everyone with the information that he was not the sole genius in our family—that, indeed, with the (I felt) obvious exception of myself we were all brainy, well connected, and important.

As we left, everyone bowed and said, "Good-by, Miss Thomas," with such grave deference that my aunt, customarily so restrained and poised, smiled, laughed, waved, and generally behaved—for the first I ever saw her—like a woman.

Then, one afternoon, with a casual, patently deceitful air that instantly set me on the alert, my aunt persuaded Miss Jones to go along with us to Miss Kopestonsky's room.

When we entered, I saw that the room's shades had been drawn and there was a dimness everywhere. What with Miss Kopestonsky's figure stretched out before us on the bed, I was reminded of the viewing of a corpse to which my mother had once taken me. Was Miss Kopestonsky dead? I was so occupied by this question that I did not notice my father standing by the window. He looked as if he had just finished saying something murderous, something terrible enough to have induced rigor mortis in Miss Kopestonsky's habitually restless shape.

My aunt, coming to a halt, said nothing. She seemed to have forgotten the flowers, which lay as limp as dirty linen in her right arm.

I, naturally, was a mere spectator.

Thus it was up to Miss Jones to do the talking. Almost as tipsy on tea as if she had been sipping cocktails (a reaction to that supposedly innocuous drink that I have since observed several times), she rose to the social challenge with all the skill of a Baltimore belle. Painted like a rose, her mouth opened—and out poured a display of Southern charm that I am able to compare to nothing but arias I have heard at the opera. It was the most brilliant and most brilliantly ornamented, if also the most banal, I ever listened to: she sang of "our" patient, of the weather, of anything and everything that did not matter and was not apropos. She went so far as to tell a joke about a surgeon ("You know whom I mean, Charles") who mislaid a scalpel in a lady's insides. She had us all, even my aunt, giggling and laughing and ready to applaud her . . . until, so swiftly that I did not see it until after it had happened, my father walked across the room and hugged her. He hugged her, I think, out of sheer delight in her good humor, so different than our glum Thomas moods, than Miss Kopestonsky's violent despondency. I believe I could have hugged her for the same reason. Miss Kopestonsky, however, did not appreciate either Miss Jones or my father's hugging her. She charged out of her sickly lethargy, sat up in an explosion of pink ostrich feathers and lace, raised one hand, and pointed one finger at Miss Jones. "Out!" she screamed. "Get out of this room this very minute!"

Her outburst astonished us all, except, I am certain, my aunt, who observed it with a shrewd and calculating eye and, in one corner of her mouth, an infinitesimal smile that could only have been triumph.

"Out!" Miss Kopestonsky said again. She was actually standing on her bed: a huge and ruffled pink bird, an ostrich. "Out, I say! Out!"

At this moment I chanced to look at my aunt again. She was watching my father, Miss Jones, and Miss Kopestonsky, each in turn, with the strangest eyes I have ever seen. For a minute her watching was all that was happening.

Then, with a shrug and a sigh, Miss Jones turned and left the room in a crackle of starch. My father gave Miss Kopestonsky a glance that she parried with one just as sharp, just as hateful; then he left. Still standing on her bed, she glowered down at Aunt Margaret and me. "You, too!" she said. Whereupon my aunt and I left.

When we got home, we were still carrying our bouquets. They were dead.

I implied, I am aware, that my aunt brought about this nasty scene in Miss Kopestonsky's hospital room. This is not to credit myself with precocious intuition and insight.

I know she brought it about because that night, as they strolled in the lightless garden, she confessed as much to my mother.

"Nancy Jones?" my mother said in a voice of trembling shock.

"The head nurse," Aunt Margaret said.

"But Margaret! Nancy Jones! Don't you remember what I told you about her?"

"No, I do not."

"That time after Charlie J came and I had to go to the hospital for repairs?"

"No."

"Well, I did tell you. I know I told you. You have just found it convenient to put it out of your mind." My mother recited the old story—the beginning, I always felt, of her tragedy—which had the identical plot as the happenings of the afternoon except that in place of Miss Kopestonsky ordering my father and Miss Jones out of the room it had been she. "Now you remember, don't you?" she said.

My aunt sounded amazed, pained. "Yes," she finally said, "now I remember your telling me about it."

"I was always suspicious of Nancy Jones," my mother said. "Did you realize she paints her face?"

"No," said my aunt.

"And she smokes cigarettes! Just like a man!"

"No," said my aunt.

"And all this sexual intrigue," my mother said. "It was the most painful thing I had to go through in my tragedy. It was so painful, so excruciating, that I don't care what Nina Kopestonsky has done to me and my two fatherless boys, I pity her. I know how she must have felt to have to see Charles putting his arms around that woman, and you should not have done it, Margaret, really you shouldn't. And you call yourself a Christian!"

For the first time my mother challenged my aunt, and for the first time my aunt had nothing to say, not even in defense of her purpose. She just kept on walking, her feet crunching old leaves. I could not see her, try as I did, not only because the garden had grown so dark but also because, in and around the rhododendron bush where I was lurking, spiders had woven so many webs that the hair of my head was swathed in them, and so were my ears, nose, mouth, and eyes.

Brooding over my mother's judgment of my aunt's behavior, which, conscious or unconscious, had certainly punished Miss Kopestonsky for her depredations, I decided she was right. My aunt had caused her longtime friend a great deal of pain. I had seen the pain, the terrible spasm of muscles upon her sad and unattractive face—I had seen it in the whites of her somewhat slanty eyes. I had heard it, like a subliminal scream, in her furious repetition of the word "Out!"

At that time in my young life, I did not enjoy giving pain to any creature or creation in the world. I have mentioned my sorrow for flowers cut to decorate our dining table. I also grieved for flies trapped behind windowpanes, for ants stepped on by accident, for dogs and cats without homes. And so with Miss Kopestonsky. Mongrel though she was, she deserved my pity, I felt, since she was merely another living creature, no more unlike me than everything else that existed on earth: pale-green moths, fireflies, blades of grass. On the very night of the day Aunt Margaret had gotten her revenge on Miss Kopestonsky, I made up my mind to do something to make her feel better.

Next day, without notifying either my mother or aunt of my plans, I went by myself to the hospital. I went early in order to avoid my father. I used the back stairs and minor corridors where I was not likely to run into Miss Jones.

Pushing open the half-door, which had an opaque, pleated beige curtain, I entered Miss Kopestonsky's room without knocking. She was still wearing her pink-feathered bed-jacket. She appeared to be sleeping. I tiptoed toward her, holding out a tiny bunch of sweetly-peppery red carnations that I had bought for a quarter at a flower stand in the crisscross of shadows on Market Street. The carnations—six of them, I think—were as red as if I were handing over my heart and innards.

Although Miss Kopestonsky's wrinkled eyelids appeared to be closed, remaining as motionless as lizards in a nook of sunlight, she was actually watching me. When I arrived almost within reaching distance of the bed, which had never seemed so high, she said, "And what do *you* want?" her lips opening, it seemed to me, only after she had pronounced those unexpected words, and her eyes opening only after that.

Presenting my bouquet, I said, "Miss Kopestonsky, I thought you might like these," realizing, even as I spoke in my rather priggish, goody-goody fashion, how skimpy the carnations looked in that wilting bower all around her.

Instead of accepting them for what they were worth—which was something, considering that I was the one person in our family to have felt sympathy for her difficult position—she suddenly raised a hand and struck the car-

81

nations out of my Little Lord Fauntleroy grasp. They fell to the floor and lay there like a puddle of blood I had seen once in the accident ward many floors below.

Surprised, I suspect, by her own impetuous and violent act, she lay back on the low pile of white-cased pillows and audibly caught her breath and finally said to me:

"What do I want your sympathy for? I am not interested in you. I didn't bargain for a family. I don't want to see you—*or* your baby brother—*or* your aunt. Just stay away from me, all of you! And from your father too. Because, young man—I hate to tell you—your father doesn't care about you any more than I do. Less, really, if you want to know the truth."

At the moment, her rudeness more than her fury or the awful meaning of her words took me thoroughly aback. Socially embarrassed, I was able to think and do nothing but make a bow of farewell, a bending of the waist of the little-gentleman variety that was promoted at my weekly dancing class. I made the bow, if I do say so, with elegance and poise.

Then I departed. . . .

Never until now, which is to say for four decades, have I told anyone about my solo trip to town—neither my mother, hidden in her garden of grief, nor my aunt, who grew disturbingly silent, like a general reassessing strategies, as she began for the first time to doubt the means she had adopted to accomplish her unshakable purpose, the mission He had given her to perform.

CHAPTER

FOUR

Along with her conscience—which I had always imagined as sounding exactly like Grandma Thomas—my aunt had to cope with my mother. My mother intransigently refused to give up her disapproval of the scene that had taken place in Miss Kopestonsky's hospital room. It was certainly odd, this defense-to-the-death of her mortal enemy. To a person of Aunt Margaret's certainties and prides it was unbearably galling. She attempted to change it.

On the first genuinely scalding day of summer, my mother, wearing her straw hat, sat in the garden—floating there, it appeared to me, like a dead fish washed up among

83

other debris: the rain-fractured delphinium, the rotting bergamot, the ramblers red and dying. The heat never ebbed. At my listening and watching post within the dark green damp and shade of a rhododendron, I alternately stared and dozed. Then, with a stride and a swing of her arms, my aunt braved the garden. She came to a halt directly over my mother and, glaring down at her, said, "I know you didn't mean what you said the other night, Star. You couldn't possibly have."

My mother's mouth opened and shut several times. "Meant what about what?"

"About Nina and Charles and that nurse. And me."

"I did mean it, Margaret."

"But how could you have possibly meant it, Star? You know that whatever I do is done for you and the boys."

My mother's eyes remained blue and white and dull.

"Why else would I do such a thing?" said my aunt.

"I don't know, Margaret," my mother said, "I'm sure I don't know." And then she did move. Not extravagantly. Not angrily. She made a fanlike spread of her unusually white hands—I have seen photographs of the Pope on a balcony employing the identical gesture.

"Why are you carrying on so, Margaret?" she asked. "I have finally admitted to myself that Charles and I are over and done with. Why can't you? All I want now is to forget. Why don't you? What do you know about it, anyway? Have you ever loved another human being? What do you know about anything except this vague creature somewhere up in the sky whom you call God?"

My aunt maintained her stiff and commanding attitude in the face of my mother's uncharacteristic attack. If I remember correctly, she shook her head slightly. Her black hair glistened like steel in the downpour of June sunlight that allowed no shadows anywhere except within the cell-like, well-barred confines of my rhododendron. The air was too thick and too hot to breathe, and my aunt waited perhaps a full minute before she replied: "You may be right, Star. Maybe I don't know anything about what you so smugly call love. If so, it hasn't been my fault. God knows. God knows everything, and I leave the final judgment to Him. According to my thinking, though, all I have done is what He summoned me here to your house to do, and I am sorry—I am very, very sorry—to hear you taking His name in vain!"

And then for the first time since the previous autumn, my mother performed an act that was truly characteristic, much more like her than the trance-like melancholy in which she had sat eating marshmallows all winter long. She was, as I have said, so young, so fresh in her feelings, so naive of mind. Like most children, she did not care to be treated as a child. She resented my aunt's doing it. She lost her temper. She pulled the brim of her straw hat down over her rash-spotted forehead, gathered up her still unused clippers and trowel, got to her feet, and walked off with a girlish gait that swung to and fro as if she were still wearing the long skirts of the turn of the century. She disappeared, saying, "I don't care, Margaret! I don't care! I'm going to the porch and have a glass of tea!"

For her, I see now, it was the beginning of her recovery. After that day, which must have been near the end of June, she did not go back to the garden to brood over my father and Miss Kopestonsky. With glass after glass of cloudily red iced tea replacing her diet of marshmallows, and with book after book from the local gift shop, which had a rental library, supplanting her tragedy with fictional ones, she stayed on the swing in the ever-fluttering shade of the blue clematis on our front porch.

My mother's dissent irritated Aunt Margaret. It must have contributed a doubt to her hyperactive mind—a doubt that only angered her more by being in the path of her single purpose. By no expression on her face, however, nor by any overt gesture of her body did she give away her feelings.

I watched her continuously. All I could feel sure of was the permanency of her purpose: she could not rid herself of it or of her conviction that it was the Will of God without losing her own self. She did more typewriting than ever before. The clog-dance of her card table pounded in our ears downstairs in the same way that her purpose must have been pounding in her veins and nerves, in the painful intensities of her consciousness. She grew exceedingly nervous. Her hands shook. She chewed each mouthful of her food with raging mathematics, forty mastications, no more no less, to each bite. Her eyes turned blacker. Her gaze turned into a stare, inscrutable, impenetrable, hard to bear: sometimes it fixed on me—across the table, say—as if I were not really there.

One day, as I lay and observed her from my burrow of damp, brownish, white-veined, insect-eaten leaves on the edge of the garden, I happened to see a most surprising scene. A bee—one of the big black-and-yellow-striped variety that thronged the lavender cones of our butterfly bush—suddenly flew like a bullet and struck her on the left

86

side of her bosom. I saw that it hurt her. Yet she only gave a harsh start, glanced down at the attacker, which resembled a brooch attached to her blouse, smashed it dead with a single slap of her hand, and brushed it off so that it dropped to the limp grass at her feet. Next, she opened four buttons down the front of her white blouse, and inspected the bitten spot on her amber-tinted bare skin. I was able to see everything. It was the first I knew that she had no breasts whatever.

The fact fascinated me. I went upstairs to my room and looked at myself nude in the mirror. Aunt Margaret and I were the same! In order to verify this mystery, I waited until the hour when she drew her daily bath. I put my eye to the keyhole of the bathroom. Useless. A key was in it— the door was locked. I moved to the so-called "ironing room" across the second-floor hall and hid myself behind wicker baskets full of dirty clothes waiting for Patience to wash them, my scheme being to spy on my aunt from there as she left the bathroom. Also useless. As she came out, she was clad in a dressing gown and the full length of her loose hair. I was kept awake that night by puzzlement. Eventually I climbed out of bed and went back to the garden, the site of my interesting and baffling discovery, in hopes of living through it again.

I wandered over the grass, which to my bare feet felt as warm as ashes, dark though the night was.

The garden, now grown so tall, as tall in some places as my father himself, was unusually black, so black that the sky shone a surprising blue, with many stars in it, reddish, gold, but mostly white. Several I saw fall, each one dripping downward toward the garden as slowly as molten wax, but each one before it disappeared bursting out with one final yellow flare, like the last burst of a Roman candle on the Fourth of July.

I sought comfort by stretching out on the grass between the flower beds. But the grass was too scratchy against my naked back. Moreover, my excitement over my aunt's anatomical similarity to myself, as I mulled it over, increased instead of diminishing. I rolled over and over as restlessly as if I had stayed in bed in my airless room upstairs. Eventually I went back to my rhododendron bush, which, while no breezier or cooler, offered as my sheet that wet mulch of ancient leaves and as my pillow a damp, smooth stone that by daylight shone silvery. After indulging in my bad habit, of which I was as ashamed as a character out of Hawthorne, I went to sleep.

I was wakened, I don't know at what hour of that extraordinarily jungle-like darkness, by the arrival of someone. Footsteps roused me. I heard them strolling, pausing here and there and then proceeding in an apparently aimless tour of the flowers.

I was on the alert immediately.

Soon, against the astonishing stars and blueness of the sky, I made out the silhouette of our new maid Patience— Patience without her clothes, her dark skin darker than the darkness but glittering like metal, like brass, as if she were a statue mobilized. She was the same size, almost exactly, as I. Her legs were shaped like mine, which is to say they were as straight as sticks. Her hips too. I could not see the place lower down, try as I would. But, above her stomach, which was plumper than my own and longer and pear-round, she had breasts the way a woman, I knew, was supposed to. They tipped upward—like ice-cream cones, like the flowers of the butterfly bush always being drunk from by butterflies and those large dangerous bees. They were stuck onto Patience where Aunt Margaret and I were equally flat. I studied them as if they were the first I had ever seen, though, in fact, I had often spied on my mother when, believing herself alone, she sat naked but for a string of babyish seed pearls in front of her dressing table's white-framed oval mirror.

What I mistook for the flare of another falling star was the ember at the end of a cigarette in Patience's mouth. The fumes of it gave me the same immoral thrill as the reek of Miss Nancy Jones's uniform. I watched her smoke it down to all but nothing, then grind it out on the trunk of one of our maples and then shred the remnants into bits and sprinkle them so that no one from our conservative household would ever find them. Then she went indoors.

Next morning when I saw her in the kitchen, neat, busy, and silent, I was unable to connect her with the shiny metal statue I had seen in the night.

It did not occur to me that the reason Patience had gone for a walk in the all-together was the stifling atmosphere of her room, lodged in the rear of the second floor between the second and unused guestroom and the back stairs. I assumed she was being bad. Because I wanted to see her naked and smoking again (I don't know which of the two sins aroused me the more), I returned to the garden on the following night.

Again, very late, she appeared. This time, though, she was fully clothed. My joy was confined to the odor and on-and-off signal of the glowing cigarette between her lips.

Then, so unexpectedly that I did not have time to duck deeper into my cover of leathery leaves, someone else showed up, someone stealthy but heavy-footed, someone taller by far than anyone I knew, someone as dark as Patience herself as she stood there smoking and, as I now perceived, waiting for this someone underneath the meadow of flowering stars.

It was a man. A black man. Seeing him at precisely the same instant I did, Patience spread out her arms and uttered his name—"Al!"—, breathing it out along with a puff of smoke as visible as the balloon of frost in which I once saw Miss Kopestonsky speak. Al walked directly into Patience's outspread arms. They closed around him—around the white shirt that was really all I could make out of him other than the night blackness where his hands and neck and face ought to have been. They clutched him in the same complete way that the branches of our wisteria embraced our house, its shutters, clapboards, even its very stones.

I was frightened. My impulse was to run into the house and tattle on them to Mother. No doubt my fear was based on the fact that never in my life had I seen a man and a woman welcoming each other with delight and happiness.

I didn't run because simultaneously with my fear I had the thought that, if I waited, Patience might take off her dress again and Al might remove his shirt and then I would have the two of them, stark naked, to ogle, to ponder and wonder about. Having never seen my father minus his clothes—he was, oddly, as pruriently modest as he was unabashedly vain—, I was curious to find out just how big Al was, down there, compared to me.

Instead of disrobing, after wrapping Al in her creeper-like arms, Patience started to push him away. "Not here, dummy," she whispered. "They see us here, dummy. Now you stop that, dummy! Hear?"

Al held onto her.

So Patience said, "You a real dummy, ain't you, dummy?" She kept on pushing him until she, that child-sized girl versus that enormous white shirt, won the match. Al gave in, standing back from her and puffing.

"I tol' you to stay away from here," Patience said in that peculiar whisper of hers like a cat's hiss. "You done fixed me up enough. I got to keep this place, where they's payin' me seven dollars a week and my own room and bath. So git, dummy! Git!"

So similar to Miss Kopestonsky's use of the word "Out!" Patience's word "Git!" did not have a similar inflection. It was neither hateful nor unkind. It only sounded very determined—and as scared as the feelings inside me.

Al walked away as Patience told him to. He passed through a fence of clipped blue spruce, which by the brilliance of starlight looked as white as if it were laden with snow. He went through our next-door neighbors' yard and never—that I know of (and I would have known)—came back.

The next morning, when Patience's little hands, not as big as my own, served me my bowl of Corn Flakes, I could not believe they had fought off the huge, tall black man she called Al. I gaped at her hands as if they were starfish or monkey paws, guaranteed genuine oddities.

"Mother," I said later that day, "do you know what?"

"No, dear. What? You must excuse Mother, dear. Her mind was on her book."

"Patience goes to the garden every night."

"I hope she does, dear. That tiny room of hers must get unbearable on nights like the ones we've been having. Whenever her work is done, Patience can go wherever she likes—to the garden, the porch, anywhere. This is her home, too, you know."

"Even to smoke cigarettes and walk around without a stitch on?"

"Patience doesn't smoke, dear. Nice girls don't smoke. And I'm sure she doesn't walk around without a stitch on, either. You let your imagination run away with you, Charlie J. You always do. Now, don't bother Mother, dear. She wants to sit here in the nice shade and read her book and sip her iced tea in peace."

This was the sole period in my life when my mother and I, natural allies, were unable to talk with each other. Her mind was not, as she claimed, "on her book," that cellophane-bound volume from the rental library. It was, as I very well knew, much further away than that: namely on my father in his office on Chestnut Street in West Philadelphia, thirty minutes distant by car or Yellow Cab, an hour and a half by trolley, and I was jealous of her disguised concentration on my father. I suffered from her inattention.

Yet I had many activities to keep me occupied: ferns and wild flowers to press between the pages of *The Book of Knowledge*, plays to stage in the basement on rainy afternoons, a tent to construct, Japanese beetles to liberate on the sly, along with the fireflies from my brother's prison-like row of Mason jars, *Treasure Island* to reread, watercolors to paint. Best of all, more interesting to me than any fiction, I had the story of my aunt to follow day by day.

The hard time I had in pursuing Patience's tale to its end, which affected me almost as if it happened to me, was the result of one simple fact. This was that her room, almost as small as a nest, was situated so that I could not keep an eye upon her when she was there. Thus the secrets of her existence were revealed to me solely after dark when she strolled to Mother's garden to smoke the single Old Gold cigarette she allotted herself per day.

It was difficult to see her in the June darkness. Nor was there—for a time after her boy friend's final visit—much to see. There was no scene, no nakedness. There was occasionally her flat-nosed, full-lipped, small-chinned, extremely young-looking profile against the pasture of stars, but usually nothing more than the fire of her cigarette glowing steadily like a nasturtium that bloomed by night or darting on and off like some phosphorescent insect, some phosphorescent bird. . . .

And then one night, one of the brightest, so bright the northern lights must have been flickering in the back part of the sky, blowing white and silver and even pink like the undersides of starlight, my assiduity in waiting got its reward. Something happened.

It happened late. It must have been past midnight because, according to her habit, my aunt had gone to bed and gotten up to go to the bathroom and gone back to sleep again. I was ready to give up my hope of something happening that night, of Patience taking another walk without any clothes, of her having another importunate visitor. . . . Then she came. Quietly. Making no sound at all on the dry, still uncut lawn. As she walked, she smoked. I remember the remarkable duration of the redness at her mouth that night. Each time she sucked in a puff, it lasted as long as the saddest sigh, the most troublesome thought. A cricket was singing. A cicada clicking. A rabbit—a squirrel—something—stirring. The trees were as silent as darkened tents. For the first and only time I ever saw, Patience smoked two Old Golds.

Then, before the second cigarette burned out, she started, with this strange slowness, and with that red flower between her teeth, to perform what looked to me like a pagan dance, some ritual of which I had seen photographs in *The National Geographic* magazine. She raised her arms over her head and made weaving supplicating gestures. Her head swayed in time with them. Her shoulders too. And lower down. She was exceedingly graceful.

Gradually, as I incautiously lifted myself out of the long grass that bordered the rhododendron, her gracefulness turned into violence. It reminded me of her wrestling match with the man she called Al. She was leaping. Jumping. Feet stomping the ground. Thudding. Breathing like an old cow switched by Grandma Thomas to get a move on. I expected her to drop. Instead, she leaped higher and higher and more and more breathlessly until the suction of air into her gyrating body sounded like a scream. Actually, it was a scream.

At the instant I was able to define the noise for what it was, however, I was wholly captivated by the sight of her dervish arms falling out of the brightly-dark sky where her fingers had seemed a moment before to be playing with stars like pebbles. Though the scream did not stop, she was pressing the back of one of her hands to her mouth and holding it there, dancing all the while faster and faster until the fiery explosion inside her would not be contained any longer and it burst forth—what it was, I did not know. Then the scream did stop and her arms seemed to be pulling the stars down over her head like a shower of apple blossoms. Except that really it was she herself who fell, and the dance ended, leaving her without a breath that I could hear in the dapple of summer chiaroscuro cast by the aurora borealis and the huge oak and the still grasses and all our tall delphiniums.

What had happened to her? Had she danced herself to death, as I had read somewhere that someone had done? Her silence frightened me back into cover. I waited among the chill leaves. The sky flickered its mild hues, though there was no wind.

Finally she sat up. Stood up. Her hands inspected her skirt all the way down to its hem and then in back and along the sides. They stopped at a certain place, appearing to try to understand like a blind person what they felt. She bent over to look at that certain place, which I imagined I could make out now as particularly dark, as dark as the flesh of her hands or the man called Al's. She studied the certain place as if it were a book. Next, she got down on her hands and knees and began to feel the grass and the border of candytuft and coral bells. I guessed she had lost something: a ring, although I had never noticed one on her monkey fingers; a handkerchief, although I had never seen her carry one; maybe some souvenir or keepsake she wore under her dress where I could not know of its existence. She hunted everywhere within the radius of her reach.

Finally she found something. Her hands touched it and moved up off and away from it as if in fear or disgust. Whatever it was, she gathered it up, using both hands, stood again and ran with it as if it were water that could seep between her fingers, carrying it to the wire basket behind the rhododendron where we burned our daily trash. There she dropped it into the basket's residue of black ashes, shards of glass, rusty tin cans. Squatting beside the incinerator, she lighted a match and tried to start a fire within it. She struck six matches. None caught. She hesitated. She glanced around, toward our house, toward the neighbors', up at the sky. She must have seen that the night was waning. Her hesitation ceased. She leaned over and with both hands reached into the incinerator and took out of it whatever she had deposited in it. Again she glanced around. The night was paling. One star gaped. She started to run. She ran directly past me inside my rhododendron. She entered the house by the back door. She went up the back stairs. A yellow square was switched on in the extra bathroom, which she was permitted to use. The toilet was flushed six, seven, eight, I don't know precisely how many times. Then the square of light was turned off. The house was as dark again as if everybody in it—my mother, brother, aunt, and Patience herself—were as insentient as corpses. She must have gone to her minuscule room, which was papered with blue and white forget-me-nots, and climbed into her little bed with the ivory-painted head- and foot-boards and rested until morning.

When the sun came up, I sneaked out of the rhododen- dron and walked to the place where she had performed her heathenish dance. The grass and the flowers of the border had been smashed as flat as a carpet—a Persian carpet, green interwoven with finest threads of pink, white, palest blue. What I did not expect to see was the red. Red all shiny like paint. Blood! It really was blood. I gawked at it. There was as much of it as if a murder had been committed.

It was the mystery of the sight, so inexplicable, so un-expected, that bothered me rather than the gore, which was no redder than what was left on a tree stump after Grandpa Thomas chopped off the heads of half-a-dozen fryers for Sunday dinner up on his farm in Somersdale. I retreated to the depths of my rhododendron to try to figure out where the blood had come from and why.

As soon as I dared, I went to the kitchen. Patience was there, wearing a clean dress, wearing—it struck me—a face so clean of trouble of any kind it looked new. She said noth-ing as she worked at the stove.

Aunt Margaret, counting the labors of her jaw on a slice of toast, gestured at me with her fork.

Obediently I set down my glass of orange juice and bowed my head in imitation of silent grace, although in fact I was thinking of nothing but the blood on the lawn and how Patience had danced it out of herself: it had come out of her, I had decided, while she was screaming.

When I lifted my head, Aunt Margaret said, "Did you thank Him for the daily bread placed before you?"

"Yes, Aunt Margaret."

"Did you tell Him you were sorry for forgetting Him?"

"Yes."

"Patience always thanks Him before she eats and before she goes to bed, doesn't she?"

"Yes'm," Patience said.

"If Patience does it regularly, don't you think you should, Charlie J, who have so much more to be thankful for?"

"Yes, Aunt Margaret."

The fatigue of the night made me irritable. So did the ordinariness of the morning that followed: the sun shone, my aunt's jaw clicked like dice, Patience went on frying bacon in a skillet, and I wanted to know what had really happened in our garden at dawn.

Patience looked as if she had passed the night in bed like any other person.

And then, raising the two-pronged fork from the skillet, she happened to catch my stare of curiosity. I believe she understood it at once, by instinct rather than by any mental deduction, as an animal would. As I kept my unabashed stare on her, the substance of her eyes turned hard and bright.

This stony look was, I now realize, fear. Fear of me. Fear of what I might know. Fear, no doubt, of what she knew she had done. As swiftly as she could, she turned aside her eyes from mine. As soon as the bacon was done, she left the kitchen. She went outside and hung on the clothesline the dress in which she had done her frenzied midnight dance. It had been washed spotless. Then she walked from my sight in the direction of the garden.

Guessing what she was up to, I devoured my breakfast and left my aunt chewing her milk: twenty-one, twenty-two, twenty-three. I went outside. I walked around the garage. Just as I had anticipated, Patience was in the garden. She was spading up the grass where I had seen the blood. She was aware that I was watching her, but did not look up. Bent over the shovel, her wood-colored forehead agleam with sweat, she went on slowly doing what seemed to her necessary. I was intimidated by her seriousness: I no more dared speak to her at that moment than I would have addressed my father while he was puncturing the bloated stomach of the old man who lived in the Spanish house in our neighborhood. I went back indoors.

My aunt was still counting: thirty-eight, thirty-nine.

Mother came downstairs, cheerier than usual. "Guess what," she said. "Patience is such a good girl she's digging up that old patch of grass in the garden that's so uneven. I hope she's found the grass seed."

Later, Patience sat in the laundry room and polished our silver, all of it given to us by grateful patients of my father's. Then she polished our stemware, holding it up to the dazzling whiteness of the daylight. It was as if she were creating the ordinariness of the day. Yet I could tell by the hunch of her back, by the tenseness of her neck and all her gestures, that she knew I was watching her.

Both she and I were scared. Although it did not seem so then, each of us was young. I scared her, no doubt, because I must have seemed the relentlessly observant embodiment of her conscience. And I was scared by the mystery of her dance, scream, and blood. I had to know what had really happened.

So I settled down to watching her as in all the previous weeks and months I had been watching my mother and aunt. Had she ever had anything to say beyond her sullen yes'ms and no'ms, I would have eavesdropped on her too. I ensconced myself in the wing chair in the living room, which, with its numerous doors, afforded me views of a portion of every room on the ground floor. I pretended to be reading *Treasure Island,* holding the worn volume close and high, although my eyes peered over the top of it as if I were suffering one of those opthalmic afflictions that give you the appearance of looking in the very opposite direction than you are. I watched her all day long.

After a few days of this, Patience came up to me in my chair. Naturally I saw her coming. I did not glance at her, however. I turned a page and gave, I thought, the impression of complete obliviousness. She stood directly in front of me, about two feet distant, little hands on her hips. She stood there, in silence, until I was obliged to look up at her. When I did, she raised a hand to her wide and shiny nose and, waggling her fingers indecently, made a snoot at me. Being a child of notorious poise (teachers used to complain to Mother that I would smile at them while being corrected), I marked my place in my book, closed it, set it on the seat beside me, and said, "What are you doing, Patience?"

"Why you stare at me?" she said.

"I'm not staring at you."

"Yes, you do! Stare, stare, stare! Nice little boys don't do that. If you don't quit, I going to tell your mama on you!"

Frizzy head tilted at a peculiar angle, she turned then and marched back to the kitchen, skirt asway in a fashion that my mother, had she seen it, would have described as "snippety."

That night, at dinner, I raised my eyes from the pink paper frills on the lamb chops on my plate and met Patience's glance again. Although she was in the act of serving Aunt Margaret her coffee, she made another snoot at me. The hasty little gesture, unnoticed by the others, caused her to spill some of the coffee, maybe only two drops of it but awfully hot, on the glistening yellowness of my aunt's shoulder where the collar of her blouse was turned back on account of the day's windless heat.

My aunt jumped up and said, "I'm scalded!"

At this, my mother also jumped up, dipped a point of her starchy napkin in her glass of ice water, and pressed it like a poultice on the smarting and already visibly red place.

My brother started to cry.

Patience left the room.

I, sitting back, expected anything, a hysterical scene, a terrible bawling out, a firing.

But within the next instant my aunt—cool about everything in the world except Jews, Roman Catholics, Miss Kopestonsky, and my father—insisted nothing was wrong. She sat down to table again. She poked the tip of one finger into our cut-crystal butter dish, covered it with butter, and smeared it on her shoulder until it shone yellow. "Just calm down, Star," she said. "Now, just calm down and finish your supper."

My mother obeyed. She told Hughie to shush, which he did at once. Then she ate two-and-a-half servings of Thousand Island pudding.

My own feeling was one of indignation. My ingrained nosiness about Patience was being frustrated, and I decided to pay no heed to her threat of telling my mother. My intention was to pass another night in the garden in order to see what I could see. But the emotions of the day forced me to behave. I must have fallen asleep at the table and been carried upstairs to bed, probably by my aunt, for next thing I knew it was morning, all blue and white and clean.

When I went downstairs, I found my mother and aunt

leaning over the kitchen table. They were reading a note written in lead pencil on a sheet of yellow paper with blue lines on it:

Dear Missus,

You and Miss Margret been very nice to me and I hate to leave such a good home with such a nice bed and nice food. I cant stay because no matter what anybody say I done nothing wrong I swear on the good book,

Sincerely your,
Patience Blames.

As I read Patience's farewell, my head reeled with guilt, for I knew that I myself was the "anybody" to whom she referred and that it had been I, all eyes always, who had driven her away.

"I just know she's gone off with the silver or something," my mother said.

But the silver—the vegetable dishes with covers, the creamer and sugar bowl, the candlesticks, the flatware—lay where it was supposed to, inside wrappings of royal-blue felt from Bailey, Banks & Biddle, in the drawers of the mahogany buffet. My mother counted every knife, fork, and spoon.

"She must have taken *something*," she said. She went for her purse: "But my money's all here."

"Patience was a good girl," said my aunt. "Once I discovered her reading my New Testament. She wanted to know why His words were printed in red."

"But why would she take off like that? In the middle of the night? Without giving me a moment's notice?"

"I'm sure there's a good explanation," said my aunt. "I'm sure He knows what it is."

I was sure He knew too.

But everybody knew it, the real explanation, by the end of the day. The toilet overflowed in the extra bathroom that Patience had used. It would not stop running even after a great deal of jiggling of its handle by my mother and some knowledgeable, though equally useless, labors with a plunger by Aunt Margaret. The plumber had to be called, and he found what was clogging it.

Although the door to the hall giving onto that small room (which my aunt, incidentally, referred to as "the w. c.") were locked against my incorrigible prying, I heard what it was. I heard, even though my mother said, "Little pitchers have big ears, Margaret, so pray keep your voice down." And what it was was the thing that Patience had attempted to burn in the incinerator and eventually carried into the house like a cupful of water leaking through her fingers. Although I could not then believe my ears, the thing was a baby, the beginnings of a real live baby, which the plumber's assistant, very young and pale-cheeked, carried out of our house in a brown paper bag.

"The poor girl," said my mother. "Why didn't she come to me? I would have seen to it that she got the proper care and found a good home for the child."

But my aunt said, "The harlot! The little whore! It's lucky for her she did take French leave. I'd like to thrash the living daylights out of her!"

Even after I had looked up the words "harlot" and "whore" in our dictionary and pondered, in the privacy of the rhododendron bush, their still unfathomable meanings, my feelings about Patience continued to be guilty.

Nothing more was ever said in our house about Patience. She disappeared forever except in the lengthening darkness of my memory, through which she still sometimes falls and flares and disappears again like the smallest and dimmest star. I maintain her memory, I suspect, because she in her predicament seems to have been as helpless a nobody as I was, at the age of eight, caught among the adult agonies around me: my mother's melancholy, my father's erratic passion, my aunt's fury.

CHAPTER

FIVE

After Patience left, I watched Aunt Margaret more closely
than ever. I could not understand how she—so "Christian"
and so "high-minded," as everybody said, so openhanded
with old women at railroad stations, and so sensitive and
kind to my own tender anxieties—had come into possession
of the knowledge of the world that her use of the bad words
"harlot" and "whore" indicated. I waited in hopes of hear-
ing her use the bad words again. She didn't. For a while I
supposed she was thinking them to herself, "whore, whore,
whore" and "harlot, harlot, harlot."

Certainly at this time she grew extremely thoughtful.

She became so preoccupied with the sights and goings-on within her mind that I compared her behavior to my own: it was as if she had found a rhododendron of her own to hide in, a garden, proliferating within herself, to observe. There were times when the typewriter would come to an abrupt halt, when her jaw clenched right in the middle of her chewing, when—halfway through an anecdote about the Patriarch of Istanbul or Gandhi or Countess Tolstoi—she lost the thread of the story and would say, "Pardon me, Star. My mind is wandering. Where was I? Oh, yes."

It was not Patience's flight—or rather, as she deemed it, Patience's wickedness—that was distracting her. No doubt the sexuality and general sordidness of Patience's tale was not conducive to her serenity of mind. But, noticing one day that she was again wearing the "dearest" ring, I realized that her thoughts were focused still on Miss Kopestonsky.

The "dearest" ring. Considering the to-dos I had watched being made over it, plus the fact that, to my taste, it was not of any notable beauty, being too large and lumpy to appear well on a feminine hand, even one of my aunt's practical short-nailed kind, I supposed it must be of inordinate monetary value. Probably it was. In addition, I guessed its sentimental value to both my aunt and Miss Kopestonsky. In back of all their quarreling I was convinced there must be a story. Later I would uncover it.

But now, as I watched my aunt nervously twisting the ring on her finger, its variously colored reflections striking my eyes, I decided it must be magical, something like Aladdin's lamp or a voodoo doll. I wondered if my aunt was casting a spell on Miss Kopestonsky as she sat across the table from me with a sharp but faraway look in her black eyes, their corners tight with concentration.

I was not surprised when, several days after Patience's disappearance, she told me that she and I were going into town that evening. We would not be going to the hospital, she added, but to my father's office. I was relieved by this information, since, following her rejection of my bouquet of carnations, I suffered some apprehension at the idea of meeting Miss Kopestonsky again.

My knees turned to jelly that evening as, passing through the empty waiting room, I spied Miss Kopestonsky awaiting us at the top of the gold-carpeted, gold-walled stairs.

My aunt showed no lack of nerve, however. Climbing the steps ahead of me, she exclaimed, "Well, do tell! All healthy again?"

"I am," said Miss Kopestonsky. "Never better."

"What was it?" my aunt asked. "Did they ever diagnose it?"

"Nerves, they decided. Just nerves."

"Poppycock!" stated my aunt.

After this exchange, which was vociferously tense, the two women embraced. From three steps below their entangled forms I wondered which would hurl the other down on top of me. But something had changed. They did not tussle. They acted as though suddenly, but genuinely, they were fond of each other. They actually kissed. And I even found myself being treated to a kiss, more formal than affectionate but nevertheless a kiss that tasted of cold cream and flowers.

I gazed up at that too-broad mouth in Miss Kopestonsky's melon-shaped face. It was, to my astonishment, smiling. It had, in fact, been transformed. It was incapable of beauty, but at this moment it glistened and grinned and

107

pleased the eye—even such a hypercritical one as my own —with another quality that I parsed then as Miss Kopestonsky's consciousness of victory over my aunt and me and recall now (probably more accurately) as a woman's happiness, the glow of a life unexpectedly lucky, satisfied, simple. She was not only smiling. Her hair was curled— crinkled as regularly as the petals of a rose. Her dress, very billowy, looked as if she had collected the petals of all the flowers my aunt and I had lugged to her bedside and had had them sewn together by the cleverest dressmaker in town. Even her perfume was floral, heavily so, like the aroma of the gardenias on the breasts of the girls I would later in life escort to proms. "Come," she said, turning away. As Aunt Margaret and I followed in her heady wake, I felt like fainting.

But that sensation derived less from her exotic reek than from my perception that my father was waiting for us in the living room.

He was waiting impatiently. When I saw him, he had his gold watch in his hand. His expression was exasperation. (There is a shade of blue, light but intense, that I always associate with his perpetual irritability.) He said precisely what I anticipated—"You're late" to my aunt and "Hello, son" to me. His voice was as disturbing to me as his glance, vibrating, setting my senses instantly on the alert, as if I were a hunted animal. When he added, "It's good of you to come, Sister. Let's you and I go into the dining room and have this thing out," I discovered with a tingle of hope as much as of alarm that instead of having as usual invited ourselves to his house we had been summoned.

He left purposefully, and my aunt followed as he

108

wished. I seated myself in the wing chair, while Miss Kopestonsky, as self-possessed as a vase of flowers, stood at a window.

She was eavesdropping as closely as I, I believe, to the voices, preponderantly my father's, that emanated like the sounds of a solemn feast from the dining room. I could make out sounds although not actual words. I could not endure this. Without excusing myself, I arose from my chair and started to leave the living room.

"Where are you going?" Miss Kopestonsky asked.

"I've got to go to the bathroom."

"Well, use the upstairs one, please. First door to your right. And come straight back. Your father does not care to be interrupted when he's got something on his mind."

I was surprised that Miss Kopestonsky permitted me to go, that she did not see through my transparent little ruse, but then, as I should have realized, she had her own deep interest in the talk being conducted at the other end of the second floor.

I tiptoed down the hall, passing the stairs to which I had been directed. I placed myself as flat as a shadow against the narrow extension of wall outside the dining room. It was dim there, although the dining room's chandeliers and sconces burned with a brightness that made it possible for me to see the reflections of my father and aunt in the glass of a tall uncurtained window immediately opposite me. Their familiar figures, reduced and silhouetted within the window's frame, composed a smallish picture—like one by Ryder—unparticularized, opaque, lurid, and strange.

They sat facing each other from the ends of the long, unset table. Neither moved. Both rested their hands in front of them. On my aunt's I saw the flowery gleams of the "dearest" ring. And it was of that intriguingly controversial adornment, keepsake, trophy, whatever it was, that my father was speaking in the deep ultramarine tones he used to secretaries, nurses, spouses of people very ill: ". . . and I must say, Sister, in my opinion Nina's right. The ring belongs to her. It does, doesn't it? It was given her by her friend, that Jean Somebody-or-other. Well, wasn't it? So it's hers, right? It seems to me the only honorable thing you can do is give it back to her."

"Listen," said my aunt without a single motion of her hands or face that I could catch in the scumble of reflections in the window across from me, "let me tell you about the ring. Jean Phillips was my friend first. When I had my breakdown, she was the one who picked me up and put me back on my feet. Don't shake your head like that, Charles. It was a breakdown just like all our brothers' and sisters'. I wasn't cut out for teaching school. All those bad boys and silly girls. I am a Thomas, after all, Charles, a Thomas born and bred. Mama did not raise any of us to be nobodies. So, whether you like it or not, Charles, it *was* a breakdown. Call it a collapse of hope, if you prefer, or one awful moment's weakening of my faith. . . ."

Although it was impossible for me to imagine my aunt suffering a loss of either her imperious hopes or her almost servantlike dutifulness toward the Lord God Almighty, it was interesting to hear that it was during this time of her life, when she was teaching school, that she had first formed her low opinion of "mind doctors." On the recommendation of Grandma Thomas, a woman much more intelligent than I ever realized while she lived, and much better read, being a devotee of *The Christian Herald* and Emerson's essays as well as of the Bible, my aunt had gone to see a psychiatrist in nearby Johnstown, an old man with a tobacco-colored mustache, whisky breath, and a way of "stating the facts," as my aunt said, that she could not abide. Later, thanks to the Almighty's sense of justice, he had been shot in a banana war. For he had done her no good. If anything he had made her worse. Her depressions deepened. Her deathlike sleeps came close to lasting forever. She could not eat. She lost weight. She grew as pale as milk. She trembled all over—as if, she said, a devil were inhabiting her. And so she had been sent away from home for a summer, to a cottage rented for her on the green and shady shore of Lake Chatauqua.

It had been beside that lake, whose water ran as blue and swift as the sky, that she had met Jean Phillips. "My dearest friend ever," she said with emphatic nostalgia. She did not have to go into Jean's lineage, which had produced many governors, many successful men of business, many personages of distinction. "The Phillipses are not country folk like us, Charles." Yet, for all the differences of their backgrounds, she and Jean had hit it off at once.

"We were like twin sisters. People sometimes asked us if we actually were. We really did look alike. And sometimes, just for fun, we dressed alike."

And Jean, too, was troubled. Spiritually troubled. For all her wealth, her swanky connections, her invitations everywhere, Jean lacked a purpose in her life. She needed something or someone to believe in.

"And so I talked to her," my aunt said. "Oh, how I talked! I talked until I was blue in the face! And when I finished, I had not only converted Jean, I had rediscovered my own faith!"

She was convinced that the Almighty had planned for

Jean and herself to meet at that particular time in each other's life in that particular place, with all the old ladies playing parchesi or shuffleboard on the white gingerbread porches. It came as a revelation. As a blinding light. "Like Saint Paul," my aunt said, "on the road to Damascus."

And so, pledging their mutual devotion to Him and the dissemination of His Word, the twin-like pair had set out on September twenty-first, seven years ago. She proceeded then (my father listening from his end of the dinner table without a word or a gesture) to tell the stories I knew so well. About the cobra in her bed in Calcutta. About the scorpion in Jean's boot at the mission station in Mombasa. About Gandhi, who had been charming. About Countess Tolstoi, who had also been charming. About the Patriarch of Istanbul, who had been less so.

Finally she reached the arrival of Nina Kopestonsky in her and Jean's life. They had come home on furlough and met her after an evening of speechmaking and questions-and-answers from the audience. In Miss Kopestonsky she and Jean had spotted the tireless capacity for work, the need of purpose, and the selflessness ("Ha!" my aunt said here) that were the minimal requirements for any-one desirous of banding together with them. And Miss Ko-pestonsky, who seems to have tried her hand at every other career, from the teaching of shorthand to the selling of undergarments in a five-and-dime, had been so desirous. Miss Kopestonsky had longed to be put to use. It had taken Jean and her but a single evening to recruit her.

"Nina was ready for us, and we, you might say, were ready for her."

In the course of gallivanting around the world, there

was much paperwork to be done, itineraries to be mapped out, visas, tickets, and accommodations to be secured, lectures to be scheduled, lecture-halls to be located, contributions to be solicited, thanks to be expressed to those who heard The Word and gave. All these chores had been turned over to Miss Kopestonsky, "who," said my aunt, "was very efficient, the perfect secretary. I'll hand her that."

With Miss Kopestonsky in charge of the details, and Jean supplying the funds, and Aunt Margaret herself looking after what she called "the over-all picture," they formed an unbeatable trio. To my aunt at least it seemed as if The Great Day were on the verge of dawning. It was the high point of her life.

How long had this bliss endured? A year? Six months? Less? It was hard for her to remember precisely, so intoxicating was such happiness.

And then suddenly—in Sparta?—Zagreb?—Passy?—where?—it came to an end. "It was all over," my aunt said, and I could hear in her low and lovely voice a perplexity such as is seldom detectable on the lips of grown-ups. "All over."

The parasite—that was the word she used so noisily it echoed, I am positive, to the living room—the parasite had worked her subtle labors. Under the influence of the parasite, Jean Phillips lost interest in The Cause. She grew bored with traveling, with the everlasting rush, the crush of people, the clatter of foreign languages. Pleading a financial setback (and, to prove the fact, going so far as to have her pet Percherons shot rather than see them sold to someone else), Jean decided to go back to the States, to her father, the ex-governor, to her house overlooking the Hudson River, to her stables, empty now of all life except her memories.

"It happened right under my nose," my aunt said, "and I was too innocent to know it or even be afraid of its happening until I saw the ring."

Again I heard Aunt Margaret's perplexity, that incredible incredulity of hers, so young, obviously so painful for her to feel.

One day—somewhere—"Yes, I remember now, it was in Paris, at Jean's apartment"—she saw it: the "dearest" ring on Miss Kopestonsky's finger. Jean had given it to her instead of to my aunt. "Yes," my aunt said, "legally, I suppose, it's Nina's. But morally—it was paid for with everything I lived for, everything I believed in on this earth (thank goodness I had Him above to be my rock), so whose is it really, Charles? I ask you."

My aunt spread out her hand. The ring glowed. In the windowpane it shone like a star. My father looked at it from the long distance of the table, which he seemed to have placed between her and himself on purpose, as if to prevent a more intimate interview, a more dangerous dialogue. He was unusually quiet, as when he listened through his stethoscope to a patient's heartbeat.

"That is why," my aunt concluded, "I will not give the ring back to Nina. In every important sense of the word, it is mine. Our Father knows it too, and wants me to have it. He has told me so in the silences of the night."

My father stayed quiet until he felt sure she had finished. Then, without raising his voice, as if he were merely prescribing aspirin or bed-rest, he said, "You will

114

give it back to Nina, Sister. And not only that. After you have given it back, you will apologize to her for taking it."

"Apologize?"

"Yes, apologize."

In my father's voice I detected at last the familiar undertones of rage, of the fury that all of us seemed destined to rile in him, my mother, my brother, and I (especially I, I felt), and now even my aunt. I was not surprised to see him rise and walk down the length of the table, his white doctor's jacket dwindling in the glass before me. He went to Aunt Margaret, placed his hand upon hers—the one, that is, that wore the "dearest" ring—and with an expert pale-knuckled twist of her fingers took it away from her. He had it. He stood there holding it. He said nothing.

Then my aunt, also silent, rose. She started to leave with that kind of shuffle I have seen, in later years, in people who have witnessed a most terrible event—an accident, a murder, an execution. It was shock, no doubt. But to me it seemed that she was at that moment retiring forever from a world in which such a thing could occur, where Wrong could not only be contemplated but be committed by her favorite brother.

She was within a step of arriving at the door from the dining room and the hall where I stood poised to run, when my father said, "And now go in to Nina and apologize."

"I will not!"

She came through the dining-room door, passing directly by me without seeing me there, her face hooded by sorrow. It was nothing but sorrow—all down-drawn lines and eyes darkly awater, the skin itself so alchemized by emotion that it appeared to be made of a substance other than human flesh. It looked like metal—like beaten gold.

She was descending the circular stairs to the waiting room in the most silent silence I have ever heard.

My father shouted her name: "Margaret!" Then: "Sister!" And then, guessing what she was doing and where she was going, he stalked out of the dining room and strode past me as blindly as she had, as he watched her figure proceeding down the stairs contrary to his command. I saw him swell up. Fury inflated him to twice his real size.

Then, as unexpectedly for him as for me, he turned, and found me spread-eagled there like a thief against the wall. His blue glare, which had been intended for my aunt, cut me instead. Then with the hand that did not contain the "dearest" ring he grabbed hold of me and propelled me as if I were made of paper in the direction of the staircase and gave me a shove. He pushed me. I tumbled pell-mell down the steps behind my aunt and was stopped from falling all the way only by the heels of her shoes.

"Oh, Charles!" she said.

I picked myself up, extricating my feet from the spindles of the gold-painted banisters.

And then he began to shout: "And take this boy out of here! He's not even a boy! He's a mollycoddle, a mama's darling, a. . . ."

I awaited, with a dignity I had taught myself just for this purpose, the word "sissy," which was his customary epithet for me. Perhaps because his temper was always short and always short-lived, and perhaps because he was already starting to be ashamed of his anger (one must remember that essentially he was a decent and extremely intelligent man), he did not say it. He might just as well have said it, however, for the word was implicit in all the words he did employ—it invariably was—and so the unuttered noun resounds in my memory to this day, even though I know for a fact he did not say it: "Sissy! Goddamn si-sssssssssssy!"

My aunt took my hand and led me out of the house. It was raining As my aunt hailed a cab, I glanced upward and saw Miss Kopestonsky, still as motionless as a vase of flowers, standing in the gold-tinted wet window on the second floor.

It was with my father's mortal though unspoken insult in my ears that I began the conscientious practice of my stillness.

I removed myself to the garden. I always took with me my copy of *Treasure Island*, my box of paints, a pad of watercoloring paper, and a banana. Sometimes I provisioned myself with a jar of peanut butter with which, halving the banana, would make a sandwich. Mainly, though, when I was in the garden, I just thought. I thought of my father's terrible word. I thought of my aunt's loss of the "dearest" ring. I thought of Miss Kopestonsky's victory over all of us—over everybody, including Jean Phillips, including my father himself. How had she managed it, that plain unexceptional woman? It seemed to me that if I thought long and hard enough about these matters, any one of which was sufficiently complex to provide me with a whole day's mental activity, I would be able to solve them like crossword puzzles: I imagined that once I had filled in all the blank spaces I would be able to discard my troubles, indifferently, as I did the page of funnies and riddles in our Sunday paper. . . .

This did not work. Maybe it was a false hope to expect it would. Maybe my thinking was faulty. For the more I set my mind to one or the other of these important matters (I would assign myself one per day, as if it were a lesson to be studied for school) the more I found to think about— mazes of thoughts; and all my labor produced nothing more than a confusion so baffling and so disturbing that one day the subject of my study was my confusion itself.

Finding my intellectual powers unequal to such mysteries, I felt obliged to give up. Whereupon I started putting every thought about every other thought out of my mind as dutifully as though I were a Christian Scientist. By this process, no doubt, my thoughts were transferred to more profound areas of my being and, from those secret storage places, continue to this day to exert their effects upon me, accounting perhaps for my hives, pimples, constipation, headaches, and muscles so taut they hurt.

Inside the rhododendron bush with its dim green privacy and deliciously rank and body-like odor of rotting leaves, I existed like one of the plants in the garden; it became my home just as it was the home of the roses, the delphiniums and the butterfly bush. I was happy because, putting aside all thoughts from my mind, I taught myself to endure with the natural contentment of a blade of grass. I was. That was enough.

My mother: "Where is Charlie J? He must be out in the garden again. He's always in the garden. I swear, if I let him, that child would spend his whole life out there!"

Sometimes, without her knowledge, I did spend nights in the garden. And it was there that I had the opportunity, the awful privilege, of seeing the penultimate events in Aunt Margaret's final breakdown.

The first night she appeared, while I was playing hooky from my bed on the overheated third floor, I mistook her for Patience—Patience come back to forgive me for my staring and knowing. The mistake lasted only a moment, not only because of the difference between the silhouettes of the two women, the one so tiny and the other looming as high and substantial as a soldier on dress parade, but also because of their different ways of moving: where the black girl had danced, my aunt plodded. This peculiar and alien weightedness, which I had glimpsed first when Aunt Margaret was going down the staircase in my father's house, had become her prime characteristic. So ponderous was the invisible burden on her that sometimes I wondered if she was physically capable of heaving herself up to the second floor to do her day's work. Even after she had reached the second floor, I would hear no jabs or pecks at the typewriter on the card table. More and more no sound would come from up there, for hours and then for days in a row.

Although I was religiously practicing the rites and trying to stick to the tenets of my stillness in the garden, I always knew what was happening. With a deepening fear and a sense of being abandoned, I knew Aunt Margaret was turning into stone. She not only walked as if she were made of stone, she also talked as if her tongue, ordinarily so quick and eloquent, had been transmuted into that element. Her words became slurred. She left sentences unfinished.

Even my mother noticed the change in her. "Are you

all right, Margaret?" she asked. "Do you need a dose of salts or something?"

"No, Star, I am fine," my aunt said. "I have surrendered myself to Him. Not my way, but His. Whatever way He leads, I shall follow, be it to the Cross or Crown."

Her inspirational words sounded like a handful of pebbles dropped onto the floor.

One night, when I was summering again in my rhododendron, she came out of the house quite late, much later than customarily, close, perhaps, to midnight. She did not see me. She did not, I had the impression, see anything. Her eyes had become stones, and she went stumbling through the black flowers and black weeds and all the black incontinent vines that, by this time of the year, had entangled themselves with everything else that grew there, including myself while I meditated or slept, sometimes taking gentle holds upon my foot, calf, wrist, throat, ear. She made one ponderous, awkward, and apparently purposeless tour of the garden and went back inside the house.

The next night she did the same. This time, being ready for her, I was able to observe her more closely. As she strolled (if that word can be used to describe her ungainly and literally unbalanced meanderings), she talked to herself. She spoke softly and rapidly, as though the message from On High that she had failed once again that day either to receive or pound out on her typewriter was pronouncing itself of its own divine volition upon her marble lips. She rattled on like a teletype machine. I could not determine whether she was addressing herself, or Jean Phillips, or the Almighty, or my father.

The night after that, having honed my ears for the purpose, I heard her more distinctly.

"Oh," she said in an oddly flat and mechanical tone, "maybe if I had developed into a woman like all the others, it wouldn't have happened."

By this remark, it occurred to me she must have been referring to her lack of breasts. I was fascinated by this disfigurement of hers, which made identification with her so easy for me. But her mind, usually so anxious to arrive at a conclusion, to glory in certitude of all the eternal verities of heaven, was wandering as irregularly as her feet, with their elephant steps among the budding marigolds, the zinnia sprouts, the shoots of crysanthemums.

Then she was talking about "the haymow," meaning, I had no doubt, the one in Grandpa Thomas's barn in Somersdale where Hughie and I and sometimes my cousin Looey played King of the Mountain:

"The haymow," she said. "But why am I always thinking about the haymow? I should be thinking of Jean. There is a sorrow I ought not let go. Or of Nina, who's another sorrow—a bitter pill. What should I be thinking about? Something. I seem to be bewildered. And confused. My thinking does not flow as it used to. I have a head full of stones."

My aunt stumbled and almost fell. To steady herself, she reached for a branch of the butterfly bush, which snapped. Again she all but fell. This time she found a strand of our wire fence that would support her balance despite its evenly spaced barbs. It was from this position, like some lady drunk's, that she went on:

"Yet what can I do but follow? Follow, and His purpose

121

will be made clear. It will be revealed as it always has been. And always will be. World without end. It's not mine to question. Mine but to follow. His to lead. Through the dark. Such a dark, dark night. It is like Africa. Like the haymow. The haymow again! I do not know why I think about it except that it was the darkest place in my life. Yet the dark is cool."

While she was speaking, she floundered her arms in the rippling black air.

"Out here," she said, "it is cooler than in my bed where I toss and turn. What makes my bones ache so and my head split? I don't have a cold. The thermometer says I don't. And aspirin has no effect. I have not felt so ill since we ate that bad meat in Bombay. And yet we pushed on then, didn't we? And we came through. I must push on now, although it was so much easier when there were two of us, even, yes, when there were three, and I don't know where I am supposed to push on to, and, oh, I am bewildered and confused. I'm afraid, at my age, of the dark! I have lost the call!"

It was extremely frightening to hear her sobs, which, doubling and then tripling, turned into a howl. (I did not know then that howling was an appropriate mode of prayer—either that or whispering.) I was able to see her clearly now in the radiant blackness. Subtly, I had crept out of the rhododendron bush, with its gleaming leaves, and had risen to my feet. Standing, I could see that she had stretched out upon the patch of new grass where my mother used to sit and think her sad but unforgiving thoughts, where Patience had performed her dance of abortion. She lay there as on a real bed, both hands folded under one cheek to form a pillow. She lay there like a

122

child younger by years than I. The sight was more disturbing to me than her words or howls, for I knew that if she were really and truly turning into the infant I saw in front of me, as helpless and useless as my brother Hughie, I would be obliged, indeed, to abide by my stillness, the one resource remaining to me.

She stirred then. And sat up. In the bottomless darkness of summer her face, turning this way and that, that and this, looked like the face of a person drowning, like the face of a person already dead whose hair continues to grow like the shadows of grasses across whitening features. Then she gazed directly upward, raised her hands still pressed together so that they looked like the famous drawing by Dürer, and called out, it seemed, past the confines of the universe: "Oh, Lord God, show me the way! Show me the way as You have always done!"

Now, whether her elocutionary voice pled more loudly than I recall or the desperation of her prayer carried more distinctly than mere decibels, I do not know, but she obtained an answer almost immediately. A light, extraordinarily white, came on. My aunt's head, with its seaweed hair, swiveled toward it. My own, of course, spun. It was—we were equally sure, she and I—the answer, the call reiterated, the revelation at last, the Word of God descending to us as visibly as white birds.

Our joint conviction endured only a moment, however. For, square in the center of the white light, appeared my mother's nightgowned and pigtailed figure. The white light, that amazing radiance, did not come at all from On High, as both my aunt and I had supposed, but from the window of the never-used guest room on the second-floor rear of our house. My mother was raising its screen. She leaned out,

123

her pigtail with its little bow of pink satin falling down over the white clapboards. She peered—without, evidently, seeing us below. "Margaret?" she finally said. "Are you there, Margaret? I thought I heard you call."

My aunt, looking like a person just shot by a bullet, stood still and said, "No, Star, I am all right. I'll be in in a minute," and then proceeded to tumble, like a person actually killed, onto the ground.

My mother, satisfied, lowered the screen and switched off the light upstairs, leaving my aunt and me in deeper darkness than I have ever seen, a darkness such as must exist in the farthest fathom of the Pacific but possibly not even there.

For minutes I stood where I was and listened to my aunt weeping from her murdered position on the patch of lawn. And then, for the first time in my eight years of existence, I understood that just as I and the roses and the delphiniums and the butterfly bush and the jack rabbit and the cardinals were, all of us, somehow the same, formed of the same stuff, feelings, and destiny, so were Aunt Margaret and I. We were neither young nor old, male nor female, aunt nor nephew. We were just the same. . . .

Tiptoeing in the fashion I employed with the animals and birds who shared the garden with me by day or night, I approached her. She saw me and was not afraid. She went on crying, her tears, which I could see by the night's shine, like a rain falling on her cheeks. I knelt beside her. Seeing that this did not frighten her either, I sat down next to her. She lay on her back, arms flung out above her head. I lifted her head, which was heavy and wet with perspiration, and placed it very very carefully, as if it were a tiny baby, on my lap. I touched it cautiously.

124

Patted it. "Be still," I finally said. "Be still, Aunt Margaret. Be still. Be still. Be still."

But my words, the simplest repetition of hers to me when I had been so upset about my father, had no effect on her. Her crying continued. Her long body writhed with spasms of tears, which, apparently because they were so many, could find no outlet except to course through her, up and down, up and down, like the waves of an ocean inside her. I could not comfort her, not by my words, not by my hand on her hair, not by my other hand's gentle stroking of her rough-skinned face.

But then I thought of it: "In two days," I said, "it will be the Fourth of July."

And this worked.

My aunt uttered a "Yes!" that sounded like a sigh.

"Say it again, Charlie J," she said.

I did: "In two days it will be the Fourth of July."

I said it over and over again until she had grown as still as all the rest of us in the garden.

CHAPTER

SIX

And then it really was the Fourth. . . .

As always, we went to Somersdale, fifty-odd miles south of Pittsburgh, for the annual reunion of the Thomases. It was my mother's hometown too, but, not caring to present herself as "a grass widow" to her childhood friends and relatives, she chose not to go along with us. In the late afternoon on the third of July she drove my aunt, brother, and me to the Baltimore & Ohio railroad station and put us on a Pullman car for the twelve-hour ride.

It was exciting, especially eating in the diner. I selected

creamed chipped beef on toast, my favorite meal. The most excitement, though, was going to bed in a lower berth, its green rep curtains buttoned against robbers and kidnapers, its windowshade drawn to a yard-wide, half-inch-deep peephole where, whenever I awoke, as I did often, I could spy on the peculiarly identical towns of Maryland, West Virginia, and southwestern Pennsylvania: all those clapboard houses, so much smaller than ours, resembling strangers asleep in the night with their blankly black windows open like mouths.

Aunt Margaret had recovered sufficiently from her night of crisis to take charge of the journey with something like her former efficiency. It was only in the matter of arranging for the porter to rouse us in time for our dawn arrival in Somersdale that she failed. (I wonder about this error of hers, hardly to be expected of so seasoned a traveler. Did she really want to go there? Did she fear the place, her own home? Had she some foreknowledge of what would happen before July the fifth had begun?) I was wakened by Grandpa Thomas's voice: "But I know they're on this train! A woman and two boys! I got this telegram!"

There was a flurry of whispers and footsteps in the curtained corridor, sleepers coughed or mumbled, then my own curtain was being unbuttoned and a pair of darkly tinted hands reached into my berth, grasped and lifted me, and suddenly we were outside: my brother in his Doctor Denten's asleep in Grandpa's arms, myself being deposited barefoot on the dewy red bricks of the Somersdale railway station, and my aunt in her dressing gown, another hand-me-down of Jean Phillips's, all wrinkled brocade and limp lace, her hair a raggedy black shawl, her skin in the unfamiliar light of that hour showing as yellow and as criss-

crossed with dark lines as chicken feet. "But Papa!" she
was saying, "I didn't do it on purpose!"

Grandpa, as usual, had nothing to say, nothing unkind,
nothing kind, either. White-headed, white-browed, white-
mustached, he handed Hughie to her and picked up our
suitcases in his big white-bristled brown hands as they
were handed out of the door of the already moving train.
He led us to his truck. It was full of empty chicken crates.
I knew that I was expected to sit, with the black knob of
the gearshift between my knees, between Grandpa's bulk
and my aunt holding my brother.

As Grandpa drove us toward the farm, roosters were
crowing, old women in faded sunbonnets were sweeping
spotless porches, and there rose, like the sweetest dust,
Somersdale's unique odor of coal soot, rainwater, grape
arbors, fields of corn.

The road skirting the town was all uphill. We seemed
to be riding in the sky, which the sun, behind us, made as
fancy and pink as one of the crocheted doilies produced by
another aunt of mine, Aunt Grace.

I was always happy to be taken on a ride. But suddenly,
as we passed Miss Annie Enck's place, where the cat
would come out and drink milk squirted warm from the
cow's teat, I remembered my chief terror connected with
Grandpa and Grandma Thomas's farm. Between me and
this terror stood Grandma—her welcome to us all, which
included a hug and a clabber-tasting kiss for each, particularly, I noticed, for Aunt Margaret, and breakfast waiting
on the bench-encircled wooden table in the kitchen. Short,
plump in the bosom, eternally out of breath, her complexion identical with my aunt's, Grandma was delighted
that before we ate I was able to recite John 3:16: "For

God so loved the world that He gave His only begotten son." This was "my" Bible verse, presented to me by her, along with a New Testament with gold-edged pages, on the occasion of my baptism long ago. She was proud of my recitation because she held inordinately high standards for people, higher than my father's for me, higher even than Aunt Margaret's for everybody. I sensed her good opinion of me, especially after Hughie flubbed his verse. Yet I did not have the courage, in front of Grandpa, to go and whisper in her freckle-dotted ear and beg her, please, to do something to help me escape my terror. Besides, I knew what her answer would be: "Stuff and nonsense, child! Don't be silly!"

We ate our breakfast, which included cold fried chicken. And then it was time for the terror.

Grandpa said, "Boys, let's go out in the yard and do our chores before the sun gets too hot."

"And I don't want any pinfeathers, Papa," Grandma said.

"Come on, boys," Grandpa said.

There was no avoiding it. There never was. Grandpa left the kitchen, stooping under the fringe of flypaper stuck all over with tiny black corpses. My brother and I followed.

Grandpa walked into the chicken yard, where there were hundreds of chickens, all White Leghorns (Grandma referred to them as "fryers"), which once a week on Saturdays he packed into crates and piled onto the truck and took to Somersdale to sell to the townspeople: the fat lady who ran the novelty shop and the man who tended the feed store, the tellers from the bank and the soda-jerk and everybody except the Amish, the thin men who wore

beards and round-brimmed black hats with long black rib-
bons and who stood in groups under the awnings on Main
Street and never bought a thing, Grandpa told me, not
even buttons.

Scattering the knee-deep white flock like snow as he
walked into it, Grandpa carefully selected four of the
chickens. He carried them by their bright yellow feet.
Their heads, with meanly white and blue eyes, tried in
vain to right themselves. One he handed to me and one to
my brother. Both of us hated all of this, the chickens' feet
as cold as snakeskin, but scratchy and hard, and their nasty
sharp beaks.

Carrying the other two chickens in one hand, Grandpa
strolled to a tree stump, partly filled in with concrete, that
stood in the middle of the yard. "Now lay yours there,
Charlie J." I placed my chicken upon the stump, which,
though it had once been a sour-cherry tree with shiny red
fruit and marauding birds, had become, within my short
memory, a butcher's block black with blood. My chicken
struggled. Grandpa soothed it with a stroke, surprisingly
gentle, of his huge hand. Then with his free hand he found
the hatchet he wore down over his back pocket where his
penknife was kept for nail paring and also his paper pad
for figuring and remembering what Grandma told him.
He raised the hatchet and with one flashing motion that I
could not help watching, he cut off the chicken's head.
Blood spurted like my feelings. I let go of its indignant feet
. . . and headless (this was my terror) it ran across the
grassy green yard and, just as it was about to enter
Grandma's bed of zinnias over the cistern, it stumbled and
fell and lay there twitching.

The terror of killing chickens was unbearable enough for

me on Sundays when there were only four or five of us for dinner, but today, on the Fourth, when so many people were coming, the whole of the Thomas family who were not dead or incarcerated on account of dementia praecox, we repeated the murder several dozen times, my brother and I alternating as executioner's assistant.

I looked at Hughie, blond and stout and short. He was shrieking. Jumping up and down. I thought he would bite off the finger he had poked like a stopper into his mouth. At that moment, on that particular Fourth of July morning, I recognized that Hughie suffered in some ways exactly as I did. It was the first and, I think, the only time I admitted him into a likeness with me and Aunt Margaret, the flowers, animals, and insects of my stillness.

From a later event of that morning I have retained a picture of Grandpa Thomas that is as clear as a photograph. He sits with widespread legs on a milking stool in the middle of the yard and dips the dead chickens into a laundry tub of steaming water. He plucks. White feathers whirl around him. In the still-rosy daylight it looks as if his enormous shock of white hair is shedding. The picture is scented, moreover. Bay Rum.

Along about noon other members of the family started to arrive. They resembled one another or Grandma or Grandpa, but I did not know them. They came from nearby places such as Confluence and Frostburg, Johnstown and Somerset. Driving up proudly in automobiles that they parked in the almost-black shade of the row of maples ornamenting the front of the farm, they were composed mostly of women—stout, not to say obese, vastly

132

red and golden women, the majority of them wearing the white lace prayer caps of the Church of the Brethren, others favoring the shinier and showier straw versions of the same, but all of them holding on their ample laps, as if they were the sacred vessels of Holy Communion, trays of wax-paper-wrapped cakes or pies or deviled eggs or other personal specialties that they prepared solely for this day and Christmas and either a wedding or a funeral. They talked and laughed a lot, their voices high and pitchless, as if they were crooning hymns in church. The men, fewer and leaner and older looking, said little—said, as I recall, nothing except what was required by politeness. They squatted facing one another underneath the maples and picked at the grass and chewed it or else they rocked on the rockers on the circular front porch that Grandma called the "piazza." Also, there were the other children, not nearly as many as the grownups, who until much later in the day kept on staring at Hughie and me always from the same distance, no matter where we walked to avoid them. Except, that is, my cousin Louis. "Looey," we called him.

Uncle George's son, the eldest grandchild and eighteen months older than I, just as I was eighteen months older than my brother, Looey was tall, overweight, palely blond, bespectacled with yellow-gold glasses. As he ambled toward us, saying, "Hello, Hughie. Hello, Charlie J," I caught and remembered his perpetual odor of sweat. I did not speak to him, since I had hated him as long as I could remember. And in order to avoid him now I turned on my heel like a haughty girl and flounced into the house full of women.

The women were still talking, still laughing. There was one, huge, with blue eyes as vivid as a wildflower, whose laughter neighed above all the others'. At the center of them all, however, the direct and unabashed focus of all their attention, was Aunt Margaret. In her navy-blue dress with white pearl buttons down the front, she held herself like an admiral before the fleet. I noticed that the women, all her kin, addressed her with respect if not with downright caution, with bucolic awe, although there was so much information to be extracted from her before she departed again for other worlds, that their quizzing grew more and more rapid, impatient, overlapping. "Is it really as hot as they say in Africa, Margaret?"

"Hotter than Somersdale."

"Did you actually meet the Pope, Margaret?"

"No. Since I knew I would be expected to curtsy to him, I felt obliged to turn down his invitation to an audience. Jean—my friend Jean Phillips, you know, whose father used to be Governor of New York—went, though, and only pretended to curtsy."

"But you did meet a lot of famous people, didn't you, Margaret? I mean, in person?"

"Scads of them."

"Name one, Margaret!"

"Well, let's see. There was the Countess Tolstoi."

"A real countess, Margaret?"

"Born and bred. And the daughter of a great believer."

"Who else?"

"Well, Mahatma Gandhi, for one."

"Did you hear that, Grace? Margaret met Gandhi!"

Fascinated by her difference from them, which was more drastic than they supposed, the women could not stop their questioning. And Aunt Margaret loved it. She put on a show for them, at times playing the role of a per-

134

sonage I guessed to be Jean Phillips essentially, at other times dramatizing a genuine self, sophisticated and sharp, that she had never had a chance to display in our sad and lonely house outside Philadelphia.

Finally Grandma said, "Now, Margaret, come help us shuck this Golden Bantam. You can talk and work at the same time."

Ashamed of my preference for the company of women and afraid that, on account of it, Grandpa might break his silence and call me a sissy, I left the house. Except for the squatting male figures underneath the sun-whitened, flittering-green umbrellas of the maple trees, I saw no one. I went to the barn. Cautiously, because I dreaded the pecking of the nesting hens and the rats that lived there, I climbed the ladder to the haymow. It was an enormous room, extremely high, its angled ceiling draped in huge cobwebs through which swallows darted like fish through a filthy aquarium. Hay was piled into two mountains, one either side of the room. In between was a sliding door, slightly ajar and admitting one shaft, as solid as a beam of oak, of dusty-yellow morning sunlight. I found there exactly what I expected.

Looey and my brother were lying upon the peak of the mountain of hay to my left. They faced each other, their heads exactly the same size, even though Looey's body was long and ungainly and Hughie's was short and neat, like a keg. They were sniggering together. They always sniggered together, and I instantly understood that Looey was taking my brother's esteem, such as it was, away from me. Looey did this each summer on every one of our visits to the farm. It was part of Looey's selfish, boasting nature,

135

as nervous as all the Thomases', to do this, just as it was part of Hughie's to claim the attention of anyone bigger than he. Preordained though the situation may have been, I never liked it.

So, when I spotted them up there, I had an impulse. "Let's play a game!" I shouted. Grabbing a pitchfork from among several hung on the wall near the ladder, I brandished it and announced, "I am king of the mountain!" Although the hay was gray and slippery as old snow, and although I was scared of the swallows that seemed as they dipped at me to be interested in pecking the eyes out of my head, I stormed the height of the mountain of hay to my right. Standing there, pitchfork aloft, I repeated my challenge: "I am king of the mountain!"

As the eldest, tallest, strongest, and, as I once overheard my father say, "the best" of all the boys in our family, Looey could not bear to be challenged. He sat up. He glared at me across the wide bird-bothered distance of the barn. With the deliberateness that was part of his nature and also a way of swaggering, he slid down the hay across from me, chose another pitchfork from the wall near the ladder, and began with puffing earnestness to attack my mountain. He was slow and awkward, unable to keep his footing.

Long before it was of any use, I pointed my pitchfork at him, my intention being to kill him forever. I hated him. I had always hated him. I had wished to kill him even before I overheard my father's praise of him. Considering and abandoning as cowardly or sissified the thought of hurling my pitchfork down at him like an African's spear, I awaited the right moment to strike.

He stumbled again, gold-rimmed spectacles blurring in

the sunlight. But then suddenly he rose to his full height, which was superior to mine by several inches, and was standing on top of the hay in front of me.

Our duel began. We fenced with the long sun-colored tines of our pitchforks. They jingled. I parried well. All the time I could see in his eyes how he hated me. His hatred was as deadly (I now wonder why) as mine. His strokes grew stronger. Wilder. His eyes thrusting at me, too. Finally he hurled his pitchfork, spear-fashion, straight at me. I was quick, though (it was my sole advantage over him), and it flew into the hay behind me, or so I believed . . . until, on turning about, I saw it strike with a noise like a moan the forehead of my brother, who without my knowledge had been climbing up the mountain to attack me from the rear. I saw the pitchfork stuck in my brother's head. I still can see it. Actually in his forehead. On the right side, maybe an inch and a quarter above the eye. I saw the blood as well. It spurted like a chicken's. It was too much blood, it filled too generously the socket of Hughie's astonished eye, and it expressed too well my desire for a death—Looey's, my brother's, my own, by this time anybody's. I was horrified. I dropped my own pitchfork and ran sliding down the crags of hay, down the ladder, through the ground-floor corridor of empty manure-sweet stalls, out of the barn, believing as I ran that the swallows were pursuing me all the way.

For a reason I am unable to explain except perhaps that because of its leafiness it resembled the privacy of the rhododendron in my mother's garden at home, I climbed into the highest crotch of the yellow-apple tree in the yard and stayed there, hiding among the velvety-green leaves and the still-green, shining apples.

For the longest time, while I remained up in the tree, nothing happened. Finally, the kitchen screen door banged, and out came Aunt Margaret. It was as if she had a premonition of the awful happening in the haymow, for she walked directly to the barn, went in, stayed a while, and then reappeared carrying Hughie in her strong arms: the scene taking place in the silence of a nightmare while the country sun shone down on it with the intensity of noon. She stood outside the kitchen screen door with my brother in her arms. The door soon was opened for her. She went inside, while from under the maples the shadowy men rose and strolled as soft-footedly as a pack of wolves and stood together just where she had been standing looking in. Looey came sneaking out of the barn and concealed himself among them, hands in his pockets.

I assumed Hughie was dead.

Then came this yelling. Loud and babyish. And I knew he was alive. Or not dead yet.

Grandpa hurried out of the house. He took the longest strides, white hair standing out as white hair does in all directions, the tail of a white shirt flapping over his black Sunday trousers. He got into the truck, and I understood that he was going to Somersdale for the doctor.

Exactly at this moment, before Grandpa could start the truck, my father arrived from Philadelphia. His car—a new one, black with white-wall tires—stopped beside the truck. Grandpa leaned out of its cab and used his hands to talk. My father said something and got out of the car. He carried his doctor's bag. All the men turned as one and stared at him. As he walked through them, on into the kitchen, they studied him and addressed him formally as if

he were a stranger or a woman: "Good morning, Charles."
He said nothing to any of them, although he nodded—at
this one, at another or two—in the midst of his white-
coated purposefulness. He went inside.

Up in the apple tree, I was able to imagine the scene that
took place next. It would be in the library, full of Grandma's books all worn out from reading and rereading. The
red-leaved big Bible would be open on the round table to a
relevant, even consolatory, passage. The brown leather
chairs, so cool on summer days, would have been pushed
together probably by Grandma herself to form a litter to
hold my brother, whose yelling ceased, I jealously observed, as soon as my father arrived in the room. My father
would say, "Hello, son." Then he would sit down beside
Hughie. He would lay a hand, a gentle one, upon my
brother's wounded forehead. He would inspect the hole cut
by Looey's pitchfork. He would take a wad of cotton out of
his bag and douse it with alcohol and swab away the
blood, the tatters of flesh. . . .

Everybody grew quiet, the women who certainly must
have gathered at the two doors to the library, the men at
the kitchen door. I thought of them as a congregation at-
tending a service in too small a church. My father was
conducting the service. My brother's body was the altar.
There was a murmuring as of some sort of liturgical response. Then it ended. Most of the men returned to squat
under the maples, others to the rockers on the "piazza."
Only Looey stayed outside the kitchen door. He was swing-
ing in the swing where at dusk Grandma usually sat motionless except for a palm-leaf fan from the undertaker's
that she used to shoo away the heat, the flies, and midges.

Within the house the feminine talk resumed, my father's

voice joining it. He sounded to me as if he were talking to some patients. His laugh was not his real laugh. Then he came out and visited with the men on the porch and then with the men beneath the maples. With them, too, he was not natural. He shook hands with everyone, he had a word for everyone, but his sociability was brief, obviously a duty rather than a pleasure, and no one made an effort to prolong it. Finally he went to his new car, sat in it, and began writing rapidly on a pad of paper. For him, although the farm was his home and these people were his closest kin aside from Hughie and me, the car was the most comfortable place to sit, as well as being the farthest away from all of us.

The difference that day between my aunt's ease and my father's lack of it sticks in my mind. Where she submitted with good-humored egotism to the quizzing of the women, he merely went through the motions. Although I would not then have believed it, he was more alienated from his family and home than I was, even, from him. While he sat in his car jotting down notes for some future lecture or publication, one fellow, a thin red-cheeked man of about forty, dared to approach him. The fellow's hand, which had a rusty frost all over its back, rested upon the black sheen of the car window. "How's the weather been down in the city, Charles?" he asked.

My father's eyes gazed at him. "I'm doing fine, thanks, Claude," he finally said: "Took in a hundred thousand last year."

They stared at each other until, with a mumble I could not make out from my crow's-nest in the tree above them, the man named Claude walked away to rejoin the other men in the now-blue shade of the maples.

My aunt's contentment was only a braver effort to hide feelings that were even lonelier than my father's. . . .

The time came when all the food had been prepared. Minus their aprons and once again transporting their trays of wax-paper-wrapped specialities, all the women filed from the kitchen and climbed with their respective mates and offspring into the cars parked under the maples or in a circle around Grandma's "for-show" garden of red cannas and scarlet sage. Grandma and Grandpa and Aunt Margaret followed with the fried chicken, three trays of it piled high and covered also by wax paper. Looey and my brother, with a surprisingly small bandage on his forehead, trailed after them. The five of them entered the cab of the truck, one boy to the lap of each woman and on top of the boys the three trays of chicken. The truck roared. The other cars, responding immediately like wild animals, roared back. Then, with the truck leading, all the cars started their slow, formal, almost funereal procession down the road in past-noon silhouette against the high-floating all-yellow hills of Somersdale in the direction of the picnic grounds at Maple Grove.

Only then was I remembered. And it was my father, oddly enough, who remembered. I saw him in the act of remembering—the shudderlike start that put a stop to the busyness of his gold fountain pen, the swift glance around the farmyard, the irritable stepping-out from the car, the suspicious increasingly angry inspection of the fields be-

141

yond the barn and meadows across the road, and finally the call: "Charlie! Charlie J!" He moved across the lawn and stood directly under me. I spied on him as Jim Hawkins spied on his shipmates from the apple barrel. Then he felt my glance. He looked up at me straight-on. His eyes glittered, I thought, like the tines of Looey's pitchfork. He said, "What the?" And then: "Get down from there. Get down here this instant!" I did so with some trouble, since I was not an expert tree-climber to begin with and his presence always made me even more awkward. The moment my feet touched the root-roughened ground, he gave my backside a swat of his right hand. The two of us drove to the picnic grounds without speaking.

Maple Grove was precisely that: a dim, shaded, silver, brown, and green place underneath a regular planting of high trees, each with a wooden spout and a wooden bucket bound by rusty metal bands to its eaten-looking gray trunk. When we arrived, the women were spreading the food on weathered wooden tables to which benches, also wooden and gray, were nailed. The men were playing horseshoes. And the children, whom I pretended not to notice, were setting off their childish holiday toys—firecrackers and torpedoes. I looked for Looey and my brother and could not find them. Then I recalled that it was at this hour, the hottest of the hot day, just before eating, when the three of us usually went on a hunt for teaberries in a patch of May apples and dry cow-pads on the other side of the grove. Today, however, sitting in the car and still not saying a word, I did not care to join in the festivities. Nor did my father.

Aunt Margaret came up to us in the car.

"Good day, Charles," she said to my father, and I realized that she had not yet spoken to him that I knew about; they had not exchanged a word. Her purpose now, I saw, was to be pleasant. I could see the effort of it in the tight muscles of her neck, in the jerking brevity of her smile, in the unsmiling severity of her black eyes. "I'm so glad Hughie was not injured seriously," she said. "I was afraid when I found him that he really was."

"He could have been," my father said. I noticed how he tried to ignore her wish to please him, as he always did mine. He did not so much as glance up from the pad on which he was again writing in extremely blue ink with his fountain pen.

Aunt Margaret persisted where I was in the habit of giving up. She said, "And how is Nina? Well, I trust."

"She's the lucky one," my father said, still without looking up. "She doesn't have to be here today."

My aunt's face lost hold of its smile. It did not appear to know what expression to put on instead. At the same time, her hand rose and caressed the metal of the car door, which must have been as hot as an iron to touch. "Oh, Charles," she said, hand stroking and stroking, "we were so happy here—at home—when we were young."

"I wasn't," he said.

At this, my aunt stiffened and walked away, pausing at one of the feast-laden tables to filch a deviled egg, at another to snatch up a leg of fried chicken. She seemed to try to hide herself in the flock of women, although, as she should have known, she could not avoid being treated as someone special, practically a celebrity. Many women, I noticed, anxiously offered her paper plates of their specialties to sample: piccalilli, chow-chow, dumplings in chicken fat yellower than butter, slices of angel food cake, shoofly pie. She ate them all, praised them all, as polite to everybody as a ghost who does not expect mere humans to know that she does not possess an appetite.

My father stopped writing and glanced at me with eyes as blue as the ink from his pen.

"What are you sitting here for?" he said. "Why don't you go play with the other boys?"

Dutifully I left the car and went to sit against the trunk of a maple tree, the bark of which was sticky with objectionable colorless syrup. I tried to practice my stillness.

During this time of meditation, which may have lasted for a quarter of an hour, my aunt stepped out of her trance-like condition among the busy, talkative women and approached me. Since I was pretending to be oblivious of her presence, she hesitated above me. When I looked up, she appeared to have regained her normal state of being. She smiled down at me. The smile, the sweetest I have ever seen except, years before, upon my mother's face, opened up her features as though they were the petals of a flower, peculiarly fresh, pale, feminine. It was a young girl's smile. But when it spread to its fullest span and she began to speak, I heard her voice trembling.

"Charlie J," she said, "I don't want you to believe your father. He has changed. He has forgotten how it was. It was wonderful, being young here in the old days!"

I thought she was going to burst out crying. Instead, she turned away from me and walked in the opposite direction from the picnic, going so far among the rows of trees that only my keen eye was able to make her out, standing like a marble statue, and only I, I am certain, was able to guess that her tears were flowing at last, just as mine had, at my father's rejection.

Grandma decided when it was time to eat. She uttered a sort of hallooing, which, modulated and softer, she used when strolling through the chicken yard spreading handfuls of corn. When they heard it, the men and the children hurried to the tables, where the women, flapping their aprons, fans, and hands, were shooing off flies and mosquitoes and yellow jackets.

My aunt came out of the trees and took a seat at the most distant table. My father sat to Grandma's right at the central table. I found myself a place among a group of strangers, all unusually fat people with big laughs, who questioned me as to my identity: "Oh, yes, Charles's oldest."

"He favors his mother, though."

"With that coloring? He's all Thomas!"

I wanted to tell them that my eyes, gray or hazel and always changing, were identical with my mother's. But I knew that hers was the one name not to be mentioned today—hers, that is, and Miss Kopestonsky's.

We did not start to eat, needless to say, until Grandpa had said grace. Raising his monumental head (he had brushed his white hair as flat as a handkerchief), his black-lashed eyes shut, his brown-streaked white mustache aquiver, his vast hands held palms upwards and pressed together, he began, in his high baritone voice so typical of the men on my father's side of the family, to address the

145

pieces of blue sky up among the silently swaying gold-green leaves:

"Almighty God, Lord on High, Who bestowest on Thy children the bounty of this, Thy land, receive our thanks."

To me it was extremely odd to hear this mute old man's voice ringing like a church soloist's through the grove.

"We thank Thee for Thy goodness."

Recognizing the resemblance between the style of his words and Aunt Margaret's, whether they were spoken or written down, I glanced at her. She was standing at a table otherwise occupied by strangers, all dressed in black, who bowed their heads with a rigid and geometrical exactitude that, in memory, reminds me of friezes I have seen on the doors of Romanesque cathedrals, on pilasters and waterless fountains. To my surprise, my aunt's head was not bowed.

"We sing Thy praises."

Although her eyes had the intensity of prayer, she was staring at the central table, and the object of her complete attention, I instantly turned to discover, was my father, his head bowed as it was supposed to be.

"We bless Thy name, O Lord on High. Amen."

Everyone, including my aunt, who did not, however, cease her staring, replied in unison: "Amen." The word, as pronounced by fifty-some persons of all ages, resounded among the trees like the chord of a pipe organ.

"Amen," some said it twice.

I was excessively curious about my aunt's stare at my father. I longed to know exactly what it meant. But, as we seated ourselves at the tables, my curiosity about it was destroyed by my discovery that Looey and my brother had places together at the same table as my father and that they were still laughing and sniggering, my brother every once

146

in a while touching the bandage, like a badge of superiority, over his eye.

The meal went on for several hours, gluttony being the vice of the lesser members of our family (I am thinking of the fat people with whom I sat and competed for drumsticks, for cole slaw, for pickles), just as an overweening desire for perfection of the self was that of the superior ones. It was necessary for human beings of such strictness of character to have a pleasure of one kind or another. When all the food had been devoured, there was nothing for them to do but stretch out in the still-hot shade of the afternoon and doze. And snore. Everybody slept except Grandma, who was scraping serving plates, and my father, who had returned to his car, and Aunt Margaret.

Throughout the meal I kept an eye on her. Although her habit of chewing made it appear otherwise, she actually consumed very little, a piece of white meat, I think, another deviled egg, a leaf of lettuce, a spoonful of Jello. Full, she arose without excusing herself and left her table. I watched her go back into the distance of maples. She did not stand still as before. She kept on walking. She walked around and around. Around and around. When she walked to the west, she disappeared from sight in the blaze of sunlight, the blur of heat, the blackening shadows. But then, as regular as a sentry, she reappeared in the southern part of the grove and remained visible to me until once again she walked into the western view. I wondered if she was crying. I wondered if her tears were hot: I thought I saw them glinting and molten on her cheeks. And the more she kept walking and circling, walking and circling, the more, of course, I wondered why she did it, why she cried, why

147

she—the strongest of us all with the natural exception of my father—should be melting like this before my bewildered gaze. . . .

My father took out his gold watch. It caught the gleams of sunlight and shone like a mirror. Its flashing attracted Grandma's eye, and she said: "You're not going anywhere till you've shot off the fireworks."

He went back to his writing, whatever it was, in a silent, hostile obedience to her that told me a lot about the kind of boy he must have been: no better than I.

Grandpa: "Come on, Charlie J. You and I'll go ahead of the rest and set up the fireworks!"

Although I was afraid of fireworks, it was a privilege to be invited by him to set them up for the display that would take place back at the farm as soon as darkness fell completely. It was not the privilege accorded Looey and my brother when they dined at the same picnic table as my father, but it was the only privilege that had been offered me in a long time; in my gratitude for it, I poked my hand into Grandpa's. Its rough hard texture made me think of a turtle's shell. But my gesture embarrassed him. He took his hand away, pretending for the sake of my feelings to pick his nose with it. He had from nature—plus, no doubt, from a lifetime with Grandma's rigorous standards of conduct and right thinking—a stillness such as I was still trying to find. I understood this fact and the reticence that went with it. In a silence far different from that between my father and myself, he and I drove back to the farm.

Sparklers, fountains, pinwheels, Roman candles, sky

rockets, sticks of punk—everything for the display was in
readiness, under a tarp in a locked closet in the barn. The
first thing we did was roll two barrels onto the lawn in
front of the "piazza." One barrel we piled full of fireworks.
The other we left empty, its purpose being to hold the fireworks after they had been shot off. We nailed the pinwheels to the side of the barn. We lined the fountains in a
row along the driveway. We laid the sparklers in boxes on
the steps of the "piazza," available to anyone who wanted
to light one and hold it, like an exploding flower, in his
hand. Everything was ready.

Grandpa and I sat on the steps and watched the hornets
nosing the sky-colored ceiling of the "piazza." We went on
being silent together, he and I. As daylight lost its concentration and the meadow across the road turned blue and
began to fill up with mist as white as snow and the fireflies
crept out of the grass and floated higher and higher on the
surface of the incoming tide of dusk, I felt extraordinarily
safe. Of all the men in our family, I liked Grandpa best.

And then the cars began to arrive from the picnic, their
headlights stumbling toward us with the slow dumb awk-
wardness of bugs. They pulled up underneath the maples.
Aunt Margaret arrived in the first car along with Grandma
and a gentleman and his pretty wife, some Pennsylvania
Dutch connection of Grandma's from Johnstown, both of
whom remembered the flood as if it were yesterday. The
four of them walked to the "piazza" and assumed the central—I almost wrote the royal—position on the best and
softest-pillowed rockers. The rest of the family followed:
the children, who by now had lost their hostility and came
crowding to me for sparklers and sweet-smelling punk; and

149

all the grownups, including the laughing woman with the blue eye who as she settled herself beside me like a bolster on the steps finished eating a heavily frosted slice of cake and licked her fingers with a tongue as wide and pink as a cow's. My father showed up last of all, accompanied by Looey and my brother. Of that pair, my enemies, I immediately and no doubt on purpose lost track in the now dense, almost purple, darkness. I was conscious only that the entire Thomas family sat behind me, filling the "piazza" on its eastern side, where they could watch the display like tourists who have rushed to one side of a sightseeing boat in order to gape at natural wonders.

"Outen the lights in the house, someone," Grandma said. Someone did.

And then finally it was time for the display.

I was scarcely able to make out my father's figure between the two barrels in the yard before me, but when he had lit the row of fountains and they were spouting like lava or bowers of fiery blooms I was able to perceive him clearly. With my hypersensitivity to his volatile moods, I understood that, for all his natural grace as he bent to light the fountains, he was tense and hurrying. He was terribly impatient, impatient to the point of anger. He wanted to go back to Philadelphia. I believed he was anxious to return to Miss Kopestonsky but, upon mature reconsideration, I am certain he was craving to get back to work. Work, he said all his life, was his salvation: and he meant this literally—he actually imagined that an eighteen-hour day washed him clean of all his depredations.

Next came the pinwheels. Although the first fizzled and would not turn and finally sputtered out, the remaining ones created their brilliant whirligigs, blue, yellow, and white, dimming the green show put on by the fireflies.

After the pinwheels died out, a few of their flames sprouting on the black grass like crocuses, there came several minutes of such prolonged darkness that I, understanding my father so well, wondered if he had let loose his fury of boredom and uneasiness and departed without completing the display. Although I knew he would not do this if only for Grandma's sake, and although I was sure that at any instant the first rocket would fly up into the sky, I suffered a panic that was soothed only by my consciousness of the family's whispering sociability behind me, the rocking of rockers, the methodical swish of Grandma's fan.

Then, with a noise of hurtling that sounded like Looey's pitchfork flying past my ear in the haymow, a rocket rose invisibly. It was only a noise in the air until, like the beginning of the Day of Judgment as described to me by my aunt at her most rhetorical and elocutionary, a spray of the biggest stars I had ever seen, and of all colors, burst directly overhead and fell to a chorus of "Aaaaaah!" as if the artificial sight were the climax of a year's yearning by my staid and hard-working relatives—as if everyone present felt as I did, relieved and satisfied to be able to ascertain by the luridly dropping lights that my father had not, after all, gone. There he was. Still tense. Still hurrying. Still angry. He placed the burned-out rocket in the empty barrel next to the one filled with three or four dozen more rockets.

Every time my father shot one off, the same "Aaaaah!" rose over the crackling noise of its explosions. The black air reeked of gunpowder.

"Aaaaaaaaaaaaaaah!"

When the accident happened, it was more astonishing to me than the sight of Looey's pitchfork quivering like an arrow in my brother's forehead.

At first I did not know it was an accident. I heard the usual hurtling noise and sat, on the steps, awaiting the beautiful burst. Then I realized that instead of one, it was several sounds of hurtling, many of them. By the time this inexplicable fact registered upon my ears, there came the explosions of all the rockets remaining in the barrel—all of them at once. Explosions and shots of light, red, blue, green, white. Directly before my eyes. And back of me. They were bursting upon the "piazza" as if it were a fort being bombarded in history.

Grandma said, "Papa!"

He said, "Mama!"

Behind me there was such a rush and scrabbling of hands and scrambling of feet, of heavy bodies and persons running, it seemed to be one of those boys' free-for-alls at school, of which I was so frightened, when everybody piles onto everybody else. The laughing woman seated beside me placed a sticky hand on my arm and was gone. I was too scared to move. I had the sensation of being murdered. Although there was no time for a thought to be fully formed, I was convinced once again that I was the target of my father's incessant rage. It was, in the heat and darkness and blinding lights, the loneliest instant in my life so far. Maybe the victim of every murder endures such loneliness.

But then I felt a pair of arms pick me up and carry me, protected by a human chest and the lapel of a jacket, onto the porch and around the corner of the house into the safety where everyone else in the family had long ago retreated.

They all were huddling there, I think. But I recall only looking up and finding—with a unique feeling that I will preserve to the end of my days—my father's eyes gazing down at me in concern and care, in exactly the way a father's eyes always should.

By some good fortune no one had been hurt by the accident, which was obviously the immediate result of my father's impatience. It had been a shock, though, and it was not long before the whole family said good night to Grandma and left. The cars, showing red taillights, rumbled down the road.

My father stood pale under the white light in the kitchen. He said, "I'm sorry, Mama."

"Never mind. You didn't mean it," she said. She stood on tiptoe, her arms clinging to his neck as my own had done half-an-hour earlier. One tear glittered like an inappropriate and entirely uncharacteristic ornament on her yellow, brown-moled cheek. He kissed her. He took my hand then and Hughie's and led us outside to his car. My aunt said good-by next. With her, Grandma repeated her gesture exactly, the stout, short body rising on its toes to meet the kiss of her eldest child, the single tear once again briefly gleaming. Aunt Margaret followed us. Grandma stood behind the screen door, her hand raised in a dignified but quietly sorrowful wave of farewell, as though she understood that this was her last good-by to my aunt.

It was a long drive home. Even though I slept almost as soon as I had been deposited on the back seat of the car, I was spasmodically aware of many atmospheres—of the night's undiminishing heat, the country's depth of darkness, the passing lights of the towns where no one was to be seen but the phantasmal figure of a Union soldier standing at ease with his rifle atop the obelisks in the squares. Above all, I was aware of my father's fast driving: I remember thinking we must be driving sixty miles an hour all the way. . . .

I remember also my aunt saying once in a stifled voice from the front seat, "Mama's always so out of breath these days." And my father answering: "She's got angina."

And then again that silence, like the silence between Looey and me, which I immediately diagnosed as a similar mutual hatred. As I went back to sleep I wondered why they, so much more akin to each other than anyone else in the family, should hold such a feeling between them.

I do not remember what hour it was when my aunt said, "Charles, we have to talk this thing out before we get home."

"Sister," my father said, "we have nothing to say. I have only done what I had to do. There's nothing for you to do about it or say about it except accept it as a fact."

My aunt said, "Never," as once before he had uttered the same word several times to my mother on the phone.

When I awoke, we had reached my mother's house. The trees drooped with ponderous foliage. The driveway was black. At the horizon of our property my mother's garden gaped, black, deep, like the entrance to a cave. Under a sky that was dawning in rain clouds, the windows of our house looked creepily white and wrinkled, like the eyelids of unconscious people.

My father opened the door to the back seat and lifted out Hughie, while I, closing my eyes, pretended to be still asleep. He carried my brother to the front door and rang the bell.

My mother took a long time answering it. Then she appeared. Red robe. Pigtails. Face—at least as I was able to see it through the distorting isinglass windows in the car —a blur. White. A big marshmallow. Several minutes, it seemed, of astonishment at seeing my father, at seeing my brother, with his bandage, in my father's arms. And then her own arms rising in alarm. My father saying something that soothed her at once. Then his handing over my brother's shape as if he were a very expensive package from a department store.

Then I realized that up in the front seat Aunt Margaret, so relatively silent all day long except for the constant speech of her eyes, was crying again.

Maintaining my pretense of sleep, I listened to her and watched her back. At that uncolored hour, which was more the end of night than the start of day, there was little for me to see other than her silhouette, sharply outlined and atremble. She was trying, I believe, to control herself, trying, in both terror of her self and the wildest longing to let that self free, not to shake, not to utter that sound of weeping, not to express in any manner whatever the unknown urgencies of her being.

My aunt began to talk to herself. I did not quite catch all her words. I overheard "O Lord" and all the celestial imagery of her usual style, the golden stairs, the golden trumpets, the pearly gates, and other costly items so similar in their ostentation to the furnishings of my father's office.

Then—very audibly—she said, "You must stop it. Somehow," she said. "Some way."

And she gave her own answer. It was a moaning, a shriek

155

so throttled in her throat that it emerged as an echo of itself. She rocked with this sound. Her head wobbled on the usually ramrod carriage of her neck. The military feather of her hat poked at me in the back seat as Looey's pitchfork had done earlier in the day. Then by means of one vast interior effort she got hold of herself. The shaking stopped; so did the weeping; and she rested her head on the upholstery of the front seat as if she were a dying patient awaiting without hope the useless attentions of a physician.

My father came down the driveway to fetch me next. He put his hand on the handle of the rear door.

My aunt, recumbent, said, "Charles." Or rather: "Charles," her voice rising in a song whose melody and words, even, she had forgotten: "Charles."

"Yes, Sister?"

"You are not going back to that woman, Charles," she said with an inflection oddly lackadaisical, considering the vehemence of her meaning.

"I am going back to her, Sister. Nina is the only person in the world with whom I feel at home."

At this, my aunt sat straight up, the feather on her hat shaking until it broke against the roof of the car.

My father's hand left the door and reached with professional ease into the front seat. "You have let the day upset you, Sister," he said. "Come. I will take you in to Star."

In his voice there was such purpose and strength, in his outstretched hand such steadiness, that my aunt seemed for an instant to surrender her fury of feelings.

"Come, Sister."

The instant passed. My aunt's body started to writhe as if she were suffering the most awful physical pain. Her arms flew up and began to thrash and fling themselves this way and that, pummeling the upholstery, striking the glass of the windshield, scratching at the isinglass window pinned shut beside her. Her head shook in the most violent and absolute negation, until the feather on her hat, already broken, became a shredded stub that she kept on hitting against the roof.

My father opened the front door on his side of the car and with unbelievable quiet seated himself beside her. He reached over. She did not know what to expect. And before she knew it, he had a hold on her as expert as a wrestler's, restraining her shoulders and thus her arms as well. He dragged her out, underneath the steering wheel, into the morning fog that was rising like gasps of breath from the dim and greenless grass. He held her upright at the foot of the driveway. They faced each other, so alike, each of the same height precisely, of the same profile, and, in the lack of light, of the same coloring: the male and the female of the same person.

So intense was their confrontation that I did not think twice about sitting up in the back seat and watching them as openly as an audience at a theater, at a sports event.

Their pose was the formal, traditional opening of a fight. It was also a testing of the other's nerve.

My aunt was the first to give way. She dropped the pose. Or rather, it fell away from her like a petticoat, like a caul off a newborn baby. She leaned toward my father. Instead of rage she was expressing its opposite, something suddenly feminine, pleading, and gentle. I recalled her roselike smile at me back in Maple Grove. Her hands, reaching out, turned into tendrils as delicately possessive as honeysuckle. "Charles," she said in a voice I had never heard before. "Charles," she said. "Don't. I don't want you to."

157

My father took a step back from her, from the extending reach of her hands. He did not like being touched. He was, as I knew, an extremely fastidious and separate man.

"Don't," she said. "Please don't."

She advanced toward him and kept on advancing, and he retreated, step by step, so that the scene looked like a dance. Watching, I saw his face as it was hit by the first beam of the day's sunlight; it was not only pale, it was pallid with fear. He took another step backward. I could not imagine him feeling fear, yet that was what I saw in him. I observed that look with a satisfaction similar to the sensation of revenge: it was as if Aunt Margaret were relentlessly pressing my own pleas on him, my own just claims, my own unreciprocated love. . . .

Finally he stopped retreating. He stood firm. His expression changed. In a moment his face lost all fear and, despite the pallor of his cheeks, the blue of his unshaven chin, the glaze of fatigue in his eyes, he turned back into a doctor. It was the moment, I am convinced, when for the first time he understood her—his sister, my aunt.

For her it was the moment when she was all her selves at once. She was not only violent and beseeching, she was anguished. She was praying still, although her lips scarcely formed, and certainly did not pronounce aloud, whatever she was asking of the Almighty—probably, I suspect, that He stop her from doing what she was doing.

She was not stopped, however. She stepped up to my father, placed her arms in an ambiguous gesture on his shoulders, and rested her lean and wetly-handsome face upon his neck and held him, his body, as close to her as she could, considering his pillarlike stance. His features now showed horror, for her gesture—even at my age, I recognized it—was a passionate and desperate and wild and solemn and tender act of love.

At the end of an extraordinarily long moment he rescued himself from it. With superior masculine strength of body and a will power that, in this situation, anyway, showed itself more determined than hers, he broke from her embrace. He pushed her away, aside, back. And she, off balance, fell backward—in her military dress, with all its buttons shining, her hat flying off her very head, looking like a soldier not hit but shocked by the waves of an explosion close-by, her features upset not by his refusal, but by the bursting knowledge of what she in her unconscious gesture had asked of him. . . . She sprawled, all awry, on the now-glittering green of our grass.

He stood over her. He said, "Sister," the word neither angry nor loud but, as I have said, precise as a clock, intelligent and fatal: "Sister. Do you know what you are doing? Where do you think you are? Back in the haymow?"

And suddenly, at his mention of that huge and dusty place, I can see it, the first awful happening there, which must have taken place when he was not much older than I and she was in her teens. I can see it as plainly as my memory of Looey's and my battle there. The two of them lying together laughing and sniggering on top of one of the mountains of hay. The heat of another summer's day in another year long ago. The swallows darting. And then, as terrifying for him, no doubt, as the tines of Looey's pitchfork had been to me, the subtle and tremulous curiosity of her hand, that lovely tall girl's with the long, black, let-down hair. He must have lain in the most dreadful expectation while her hand explored and found him at last. She must have used him like a doll. The whole act happening in the silence and solemnity with which she had just embraced him. There is no uncertainty in my mind that this or something like it actually happened. It had to have happened to explain her behavior when he spoke to her about the haymow.

When he said it, "the haymow," she let out a scream of sudden remembrance and revelation. Her yellow hands went up like flames in the already clearing air of morning. Her hair came unpinned and fell, covering her face, and out of the hair, like the howl of some animal trapped inside its filthy burrow, the tormented scream continued.

Still standing over her, my father told her he would never be able to forget or forgive what she had done to him. She had ruined him. "Ruined," he said—and it may have been true. He told her it had been the source of unending misery for him. He grew even more explicit about its effects on her. In his cold and diagnostic mouth, which for a patient would have softened the words, he said he was sure it had been the cause of her very career itself, of her unmarried state, of her too-intimate relationships with women. "Oh, yes, Nina has told me all about you and this Jean Phillips of yours." He was sure it was the root of her devotion and submission to the Lord Himself. "The Lord is the only man you are capable of loving." Scientist, physician, man of knowledge of all the realities of human anatomy and psychology, my father confronted her, this woman whose spirit had been fashioned in the simplicities of Somersdale, with all the so-called facts of modern understanding. He heaped them on her as if he wanted to rid himself of them, so that he could stand in his own perfection and revile her.

Flat on her back, her hair down, she listened—listened as mutely as would one of the plants in my mother's garden. But then her hands arose again in the flaming air—the morning of July the fifth was as golden as if the world were on fire in God Almighty's Final Judgment of it—and she covered her hair with spatulate hands at those places where, underneath its blue-black gleaming, her ears were.

Still my father persisted. He proceeded with his diagnosis, itemizing in greater and greater detail the pathology of her case. "Your case," he said in the mechanical-sounding hatred to which I had long since grown accustomed.

So, for minutes, it went on . . . until, with the scream still spurting from her invisible mouth, Aunt Margaret got to her feet and began to run, hair afloat like a dress, and entered the house and (I could hear from the back seat of the car) raced in a panic of heels up the three flights of stairs to our topmost floor and stood there, the scream flooding down the wax-slippery steps like blood that could not be stanched.

My father followed at an amble. White-eyed from fright, my mother met him at the front door. He pushed past her and slowly mounted the stairs toward my aunt, who was standing on the uppermost step, still screaming, but more thickly now, as if the scream had clotted and begun to ooze its darkest and most necessary blood. The scream was directed, I know, at God, and at my father, and at Mother, who unconsciously laid a protective arm around my shoulders, and at me, so occupied by the sound and sight of her behavior that I did not know I had gotten out of the car and entered the house.

My father kept on climbing the stairs cautiously, repeating her name, "Margaret Thomas, Margaret Thomas,

Margaret Thomas." He was holding out his hand. . . .

The scream stopped. She tilted her head to gaze down at him, now only a few steps below her.

"Come, Margaret Thomas. Come," he said.

Her head, with hair going every which way, moved down and then up in the other direction.

"Come!" he said. He was one step away from her.

"Wait," she said.

He started to step up next to her.

"No, wait," she said, and she was fumbling with the third finger of her left hand. "There," she said. And with the grace of a femininity that took him wholly by surprise, she held the finger out to him. "Put the 'dearest' ring on." He hesitated for only an instant. Then he slid his own fingers over the one she was extending and made a motion as if he were indeed looping the ring over it. "There," he said. She gazed down at the finger and smiled, seeming to see the colorful glitter of the ring. She sighed. Then she grasped the crook of his arm, and the pair of them came walking together in happy stateliness down our uncarpeted yellow oak stairs, which, by the light of the July morning, shone as golden as those she had told me would be lowered someday from heaven. Perhaps she believed these were they; perhaps she mistook my father for the Lord or His messenger—I don't know. All I know is that when she glided past us, my mother took a step backward and so did I, and in this moment, before she smiled at me and marched out the front door, I perceived that she had achieved a stillness such as she had so lovingly urged me to seek and find and keep. I did not realize she had lost her mind, since to my voracious eyes she looked as radiant as a bride.

CHAPTER
SEVEN

"But where did Daddy take Aunt Margaret?" I asked again and again.

"To the hospital, dear," my mother finally told me.

"But she isn't sick!"

"Your father and the psychiatrist think she's sick. Very, very sick."

"The mind doctor! But she hates the mind doctor more than anybody!"

"I know, dear. But your father's convinced your Aunt Margaret's mental."

I was incapable of understanding it, my aunt's being considered "mental," which was to say "crazy"; she who was the only person besides myself to see what was what and never forget it. Her being handed over to the mind doctor was comprehensible to me solely as one more proof of my father's power, which seemed to be as great as the Almighty's. Not that I was surprised by his power or his willingness to use it. Nor that I questioned his right to it. This right—to ignore me, insult me, abandon me—I had had to enure myself to from the day of my birth.

Familiar as his rejection was, I could not and would not tolerate it. Learning to cope with it would take me another fifty years, my lifetime. And so, in the weeks after he led Aunt Margaret away as if she and not Miss Kopestonsky were going to be his bride, I minded her absence, but most of all I missed the opportunities she had given me of going into town to call on him. It did not occur to me that I could make the trip on my own volition. So I mooned around our house, which was always so hot and humid in August before the hurricanes, my desire for his company increasing along with the torpor and boredom of my days.

My mother—under the same pressure as I, but lacking the irrational stubbornness that kept me not only yearning for but expecting the impossible to happen—lapsed back into the invalid existence she had invented for herself before Aunt Margaret came to our temporary rescue. She spent her time in bed, not sleeping that I could tell (I peeped in on her, naturally), but just lying there like a limp doll, silent, meditative, frequently letting out a sigh that rattled like broken clockwork, her knuckles thrust between her regular teeth. With the deepest sigh of all she would get out of bed on occasion, put on her red bathrobe, plait the yellowing strands of her pigtail, and trudge down

164

the back stairs to cook something for me and Hughie to eat, a platter of fried mush or potato cakes or a mess of snap beans, she herself touching nothing but a marshmallow or two, her mouth getting all floury from confectioner's sugar. Her cheeks—or her forehead—would blaze with her little psychosomatic rash. Her hair would give off a disturbing reek of rose oil and nervous sweat.

Confronted by her disarray, by what I deemed her selfish concentration upon her own tragedy, I felt that she too had abandoned me. I suffered such a loneliness that, by processes deep inside me more secretive than the pulsing of my blood or the perpetual motion of my mind, I got sick and thus found an excuse to consult my father as a patient. I telephoned his office and made an appointment to see him at the first hour available on his crowded calendar.

When I showed up in my Sunday suit, his secretary said, "You're early."

"I'll read magazines," I said blithely, since already, a few steps inside the office, I felt better. Loneliness had been replaced by my hopeless hopes, and the ache in my lower left side had dwindled to a sensation of things not being quite as they were supposed to be underneath the swollen, inflamed place.

I seated myself on a leather sofa between two patients. The old gentleman to my left gave off an odor of decay that reminded me of the mulch, mildew, and dampness underneath the rhododendrons at home. On second glance, I recognized him as the patient whose orange and hairy stomach I had once watched being pierced and drained. His eyes, brown and red and quick, met mine momentarily, but he did not appear to place me or recall our previous meeting. The old lady to my right, a replica of

Grandma Grooms, my mother's mother, as upright and elegant in black and white as an Edwardian, did not notice me. No one noticed me, neither the white-jacketed assistant who imitated my father's walk, a sort of seaman's swagger that originally was Grandpa Thomas's and is now mine, nor the nurse, another woman of the lumpy and ungainly style that seemed to appeal so to my father. The secretary, having greeted me, said no more. I decided that everyone had been warned not to speak to me.

Eventually all of them left, first the patients and one by one the staff. I was alone in the waiting room, which had a gold glow. Then my father's door opened, and a whiter light flooded toward me. There he stood, taller than I remembered, and stiffer-backed, and paler-faced and bluer-jawed, a reflecting mirror on his forehead shining at me like a single eye.

"Hello, son."

From his voice and manner and stance and all his other traits that I had learned to observe with care I could tell he was going to treat me like a patient. He was being sympathetic, considerate, interested, smiling, polite, kind.

While I tiptoed over the parquet to his consulting room, I told him what was the matter with me.

"In there," he said. He pointed to a door on the far side of the consultation room. "And please remove your clothes."

"All of them?"

"All of them," he said. "If you please, sir."

In a lot less than a minute I stood naked in the so-called examining room. It was a small, high, white-painted chamber equipped with a leather-padded metal examining table, a white sink, a white scale, a white chair with an ice-cold metal seat. I shook all over and felt sick to my stomach.

My father, wearing a long white coat, sat down on a white stool in front of my mortifying nudity. "Now, say 'ah,' please, sir." The tongue depressor poked too far down my already-tense throat and I started to retch and vomit, which was one of the chief symptoms of the ailment I had described for him a minute or two before. My father's hand pushed my face toward the bowl of the sink with such rough impatience—I mistook it for disgust —that my lifelong mistrust of him stopped the abdominal uprush as instantaneously as an automatic valve. This episode, illustrating my fear as well as his rage, should have prepared both of us for what happened next day in the operating room. Be that as it may, I sat back against the freezing chair and trembled. I could see myself quaking in the mirror on his forehead, which stared at me while I stared at myself reflected in its brilliant pupil: at my puny, pale, goose-bumped skin, at the swelling on my left side, at the truss—as old-fashioned a gadget as Aunt Margaret's typewriter—that I had worn since babyhood as a result of my congenital affliction. Below, the tint of its skin growing darker, my penis was so retracted by shame and fear that it almost disappeared. I cowered over this humiliating sight. I tried to cover myself with my hands and by stooping over and crossing my legs.

"Relax, son. Nobody's going to hurt you," my father said, although already he was angry with me again. I did not know why he should be, but, looking back, I can see that his fury was directed against himself. The sight of my hernia, which had kept one of my testicles from descending, must have shown him all too clearly how he had neglected me. It was supposed to have been repaired before I started school. But then in all the hullaballoo of my childhood, first of his professional success and next of his affair with Miss Kopestonsky and our subsequent banishment to the suburbs, he had forgotten all about it, his paternal duty toward me, his mere medical responsibility. Not caring to admit any fault in himself, he felt infuriated. Turning away from me, he picked up a phone, dialed, and proceeded to bawl out my mother for not reminding him about my deformity. "You are a bad mother, Star," he said. "Instead of your children, you think only of yourself," he said. I could imagine the effect on her of these words uttered in his characteristic tone of contempt and hatred. He then told her I would enter the hospital that very evening and be operated on first thing in the morning.

It's the brightest place I've ever been, so bright I have to shut my eyes. This turns it into one of the darkest places. It has a smell as bright as the light. I think it is the smell of the light. It goes up my nose like the air in January and tingles and fills my head with brightness, forcing me to open my eyes. I blink. I can make out a lot of people, all grownups, who wear white caps and white masks so that I can see nothing except their eyes. I can tell from the eyes that some of the people are men and others women. A woman with very brown eyes is standing next to my head. I hope it is a woman because I am not afraid of women unless it is Miss Kopestonsky in one of her states. For a moment I feel some stillness. Then the woman picks up something I can barely see from the corner of my eye. I am strapped by leather belts to the table, but I can turn my head, even raise it an inch or so, and I can see it's a red rubber mask that she moves in the direction of my face. I look up into the eyes of the woman and realize that they are the eyes of a young man. I start struggling. I have freedom enough not only to bang my head but also to thrash my arms and kick my legs. Also, I can scream, which I do. Another man says something quiet. He takes the red mask and moves it toward me. I scream without pausing for breath. This brings into view my father, also capped and masked. He looks down at me as if I am inside a well. He takes the red mask. I see that his eyes are going white with rage, with hatred of me that is as old as I am, probably older. He wields the mask high. "Are you always going to be a goddamned sissy?" he yells at me. And it is he who forces the red mask and its stink of light in through the struggles of my arms and presses it down on my face, my nose, my mouth, and smothers me to death, just as I have been expecting him to do all my life. . . .

I have a dream that happens in purples. I see my mother's house. A big white dog is on the front lawn. She has two puppies playing around her. While I watch this scene, I hear my heart beating like a pump or a bass drum.

I wake up to vomit. My spew tastes of ether, of the too-bright light in the operating room. A hand touches my brow. A spoon delicately deposits a pebble of ice on my lips. My mother whispers, "Charlie J!" I open my eyes, and there she is—wearing a blue straw hat and a smile pink and rosy and prettier, even, than the one Aunt Margaret gave me at Maple Grove on the Fourth of July.

In those days the repair of an inguinal hernia was a major operation. It made me extremely sick, though I cannot be sure if its ill effects were mainly chemical, the result of ether administered to me through that red rubber mask, or psychological, the result of my father's overt desire to murder me. That that had been his intention I had no doubt whatsoever; I still do not doubt it.

As was my habit, I expressed my feelings to my mother, who, knowing me and my tendency to develop anxieties, had moved into the private room next door to mine.

"Nonsense, dear," she said. "Your father loves you. He loves us all. He just doesn't know how to show it."

"He does?" I asked.

"He does," she said. Her voice grew hard the way it did when she got angry. "He does."

"You're sure?"

"I'm sure he does—in his heart of hearts."

On the subject of my father's true feelings I had had occasion several times before this to doubt the reliability of my mother's judgment. He did, as she pointed out, visit me daily. But he did it in such a professional fashion, always surrounded by interns, graduate students, and nurses, and never saying anything personal to me, that after each of his calls I felt more certain than before that he despised me.

"In his heart of hearts," my mother said, "he loves Hughie and he loves you and he loves me."

And I could not say anything to her, because she believed all those incredible lies.

My stay in the hospital would have come to a routine end if during my second week there I had not contracted a case of whooping cough. For several days I ran a fever that was believed to be a symptom of a mild infection resulting from surgery. Then the first whoop leaped out of my mouth. It was so unexpected, so loud and violent, like an Indian's war cry, that I expected to be punished for it. My mother recognized it for what it was, however, and went to fetch a nurse, who arrived in time to hear the second whoop. So a yellow notice of quarantine was pasted on the outside of my beige-curtained door, and my mother, kissing me good-by despite all the rules of hygiene, moved out of the hospital and went home to look after Hughie, who was going to enter first grade in the fall.

Because the whoops were so strenuous, wracking my body, I had to be wrapped in adhesive tape from hip to neck to keep the incision in my side from bursting open. Thus immobilized, I had to lie in bed until the whoops stopped.

By the time this happened, summer had turned into September and I had forgotten how to walk. Every day the nurses gave me a walking lesson. I would totter like an infant from my bed to a wheel chair, one step farther every day. In the afternoons a black orderly would wheel me into one of the hospital gardens and leave me there, like a plant, in the fresh air and sunshine.

It was called a garden, but actually it was a courtyard of dried, caked, green-moulded black earth and white pebbles that spread, in the shape of a slice of pie, between two high, glass-spined walls to an iron-fenced view of Market Street and the Elevated. I was the sole occupant of this garden, which was cheerless despite a row of buttonwood trees whose foliage soaked up the golden sunlight of the hour. Close-to, the leaves of the buttonwoods were brown-stained and white, wrinkled and dead. They fell to the ground like pieces of paper. The sight of them brought on

171

a depression I was unable to break through. It felt like complete fatigue and weakness. At the same time, my mind grew hyperactive and I experienced the wildest notions. I was convinced, for instance, that I was dying of leprosy, that I had become literally untouchable thanks to this disease, and that this was the real, if still secret, reason why my mother had gone home and my father avoided me. My favorite notion, probably not so wild a one as I like to think, was that I had grown "mental" like Aunt Margaret. This seemed to be the best explanation of everything: of my sequestration in the hot and cell-like out-of-doors room every afternoon; of the iron fence; of the shards of colored glass along the tops of the walls on either side of me; of the crazily nauseating effect on my system of the sight of the buttonwood leaves being cast down all around me. And so, instead of a visit from my father, who by this time had ceased paying even his daily perfunctory call, I began to expect an interview with the mind doctor. Although I did not know what the mind doctor looked like, and although I subscribed loyally to my aunt's dread of him and his ungodly rites, I enjoyed spells of hoping that he would turn out to be as smiling, blue-eyed, and handsome as the watercolors of Jesus in my New Testament at home—a very suave and seductive person.

My walking lessons helped, and time worked its reliable therapies, and eventually I was able to get about without a wheel chair and was permitted to go to the garden whenever I liked. I began to spend whole days there. I was trying to practice my stillness. "Be still. Be still. Be still." Again and again I would repeat the simple words to myself. But they were useless. Whether it was because the garden was so ugly and overheated and really not a garden at all, or whether it was because my father continued to avoid me as religiously as though he had sworn off me for Lent (he was always swearing off something, like gravy or desserts that disagreed with him), I found no stillness within me. I would pace the scanty limits of the so-called garden like an animal in a cage.

In the course of this pacing, which I have since observed to be the habit of other inmates of other asylums, I discovered a hole in the wall to the right of the glass door as you came out of the hospital. It was an old wall, originally built of Philadelphia bricks, typically pink, rose, garnet, and black, and then reinforced by the addition of field stones and the overlay of numerous coats of cement and plaster. It reminded me of the Spanish-style wall belonging to the old man whose stomach my father had once pierced. It had the same fantastic swirls of filthy plaster and a sparse covering of some creeper that clung to it with tiny red-yellow feet like a caterpillar's. It was behind this vine that I happened to find the peephole. Not a big hole. Maybe four or five inches around, with jagged edges that crumbled, it seemed, from the force of my relentless curiosity and spilled out like white sand onto my outspread fingers.

The view the peephole provided me was of a garden almost identical to my own. It also had buttonwood trees, an iron fence, and a similar stretch of dead black earth. Its occupant was a woman. She was not an old woman, for her hair shone like a crow's feathers. She was bony and muscular and tall—or, rather, long, since my view of her was invariably horizontal: she was always stretched out on a backless wooden bench with one hand laid across her face and eyes and her other clutching a hand-picked bunch of beetle-eaten red roses that kept falling on her, petal after petal. Her skin was extremely yellow, and it was this fact that eventually permitted me to decide that the woman was Aunt Margaret. But Aunt Margaret had never lain around in that supine position. Aunt Margaret's feelings usually ended up taking the form of rage instead of this lethargy that I saw before my eyes. Yet it was she. It had to be she. Although my recognition of her meant that I must acknowledge my having become "mental" too, I was more than happy to be near her.

"Aunt Margaret!"

I tried calling to her through the peephole. For some reason she didn't hear me. When I realized this, I decided to stay at the peephole, hoping that when she sat up her glance would move to me and see me—waving—through the hole. But she never sat up. She was always recumbent, no matter how early I got to my post after breakfast, no matter how late I stayed after dark. One night I went to the garden at midnight and tried for an hour to make her out in the black silence that met my eye through the hole. I was unable to communicate with her at all.

Much as I craved it, however, communication with her was not strictly necessary. It was enough that she was there, that I was not alone. And because I was no longer alone, an occasional breeze of stillness would move across the grasses of my spirit.

I started to feel at home in my dreary garden. I would amble its triangular length. I would lean, musing, on the spikes of the iron fence. One day I was doing that when I heard a voice from Aunt Margaret's side of the wall. I rushed to the peephole. I saw a nurse standing over my aunt. "You have company," the nurse said. A second nurse, younger and stronger, rolled in a table on which a round cake of several layers filled with chocolate frosting had been placed, together with a silver knife. There were also a pair of blue plates, a pair of silver forks, and a pair of teacups on matching blue saucers. "Company!" the older nurse said again, and a tall woman wearing an excessively long fur coat strode into my view, apparently said something polite to my aunt, and then seated herself, facing her, in a wicker armchair that the second nurse supplied.

My aunt's visitor struck me as being imposing and wealthy. Her gray hair was wavily combed back from her large-nosed face and her eyes shone with that contentment, enviably spotless, unimaginably unruffled, that I have seen and been baffled by in the features of other rich people. She addressed the elder nurse, who responded with respect and immediately departed with her junior assistant. Talking all the while (I could not quite catch any of her words), the visitor then began stylishly to cut the cake. She put a decent-sized slice on each of the serving plates, poured out the two cups of tea, added lemon to one and cream to the other, and invited my aunt to partake of the little meal. My aunt sat up. I told myself it was she, all right.

My aunt liked the cake. She tasted it as though she had not been offered anything of the kind for a very long time. She devoured it, in fact, with astounding rapidity and greed, forgetting her habit of chewing every mouthful. She visibly smacked her lips and stuffed crumbs into her mouth with chocolaty fingers with which, at the same time, she impatiently and indiscriminately pushed away interfering strands of long, black, all-knotted, and uncombed hair. Her visitor cut a second slice for her. This

175

my aunt literally gobbled up too. When she asked for thirds, the visitor, whose manners were gracefully aristocratic and neat, demurred. As soon as this happened, I decided that the visitor was—had to be—my aunt's old friend and patroness, Jean Phillips. Whether she was or wasn't I had no way of knowing, but this desire of hers to control my aunt was enough to convince me that she had to be Jean Phillips. And it infuriated my aunt. Suddenly, in the midst of Jean's genteel admonishments, she stood up, hair flying, grabbed for the cake, and took it up in both hands and began to gnaw at it like a famished animal. Chocolate frosting smeared her cheeks obscenely as well as the pointy tip of her nose.

At first my aunt's visitor appeared to be frightened by such behavior. Rising, she spoke something sharp, looking irritated. Then she tried to extricate the battered cake from my aunt's grasp. Clods of it dropped to the ground like turds of excrement and squeezed in-between her fingers.

My aunt started to scream. She put back her wild-haired head and let out the scream like a howl. It reminded me oddly of the prayer she had once offered up with a similar gesture to a moonlit night in the middle of summer.

The nurses reappeared, also a couple of orderlies. Within a minute, right before my eyes, they subdued her, put a stop to her gyrations and screaming, and led her away. They led her directly past my peephole. I saw her hair all befouled with the makings of the tea party: a tea bag entangled with some strands of black hair, the mess of chocolate and pastry on her features . . . and I realized that this awful person, this lunatic, was not Aunt Margaret at

176

all. She had a general resemblance to Aunt Margaret and on the third finger of her left hand there gleamed a ring, it was true, that I had merely supposed to be the "dearest" ring. But she was not Aunt Margaret. She was only a delusion of my own crazy mind and my deep-seated longing to be near her, near someone, in this insane asylum of my own.

Next thing I knew I was being carted out of my garden by the orderly who customarily pushed my wheel chair for me. He was not much older than I. He was black-skinned and looked bruised. He had yellows instead of whites in his eyes. His name was Clarence. He could be very rough, and at this instant he treated me more roughly than usual. He carried me, kicking, to my private room and threw me upon the bed and poked his face at me and said, "Who you think you are? Huh?"

Now, I had already guessed that the reason Clarence hung around my room, sometimes doing a tap dance on the slippery floor, was that he wished to curry favor with my father by being nice to me. So my intention was to remind him of my importance, and I said in my prissiest tone: "I am Dr. Thomas's son."

"No you ain't!" He was still poking his face at me as if it were a fist. "How come if you his son," he said, "he never come to see you?"

If I had known the answer to this, I would have told him. As it was, I could only lie there and say honestly, "I don't know."

"You don't know?" Clarence said. He was doing a kind of dance of triumph. "Well, I know," he said. "He don't come to see you cause you nobody!"

177

It was true, and I knew it was true.

Whereupon Clarence reopened the curtained door, poked his head in, and said it again, "Nobody!"

After that, even if my father had stopped in to see me, Clarence would not have been there to witness the true facts of my birth. He stopped hanging around me.

It was a nurse who informed me that I was going to be taken home one day in September. I was to go by ambulance, and it was a hospital regulation that I would be pushed in the wheel chair to its red-cross-painted white door.

As we rolled down a long corridor, the nurse and I came upon a crowd outside the door of one of the private offices on the first floor. There must have been two dozen people standing on tiptoe to see through the door, nurses mostly and some interns. One said, "He's a great man." Another said, "He's a son-of-a-bitch." A third said, "One thing for sure—he'll never make a good husband."

I glanced up into the tan face of Miss Nancy Jones, the head nurse of whom both Miss Kopestonsky and my mother had been so jealous.

"What's happening, Miss Jones?"

"They're celebrating their marriage," she said in her pleasant, Southern inflection.

And then I saw, inside the white-framed door, standing together in front of a wall hung with red-sealed diplomas, my father and Miss Kopestonsky. He looked uncharacteristically shy and sheepish, hair slicked down, eyes lowered. The new bride—Miss Kopestonsky—behaved exactly like herself. She dropped her corsage of lavender orchids. She dropped her purse, also lavender and covered with seed pearls. She dropped her lavender gloves. And the turban-like decoration on her head teetered to drop too as she smiled at her wellwishers and showed her yellow teeth and said, "Thank you! Thank you! I am so happy!"

It was the first time in my life that I had to watch the triumph of mediocrity and—almost as difficult—pretend that I approved of it; but even then, at the age of eight going on nine, I was conscious of the ugliness of it. Poor Miss Kopestonsky. Rice showered her, also handfuls of confetti from several directions. But at that instant of certified victory, her canine eyes were sliding from face to face in order to measure our astonishment, envy, and malice. Finally her eyes met mine. I held them as long as they had the courage to stay there. And then she dropped. She fainted away. And my father had to pick her up and carry her through the mob of us like a fresh case for the accident ward.

The ambulance took me back to our house in the sub-urbs, where my mother welcomed me with her always-open arms. For the next ten years she would devote herself to me and my well-being. Thanks to her, I grew up into a very convincing facsimile of health and happiness.

From that year onward, however, I deemed myself either crazy like Aunt Margaret or a nobody like our maid Patience, thus adopting as my own my father's attitude toward me. During the years that followed I found no way of alleviating my sense of predestined disgrace other than the practice of my stillness. Often it did not work. But sometimes, usually at night, when mists were rising like ghostly vegetation in my mother's garden and our butterfly bush loomed like a person whom I both

yearned and feared to see there, I would repeat the prescribed words—"Be still. Be still. Be still"—and a feeling
of miraculous safety would steal over me, momentarily
imbuing my thoughts with silver.